I0682863

Hands Across the Grave

by

Donna Kolling Lear

Chapter 1

August 1967
Monrovia, California
The Home of James and Meg Riley
11:45 PM

The man stood in the shadows, watching Meg through the translucent kitchen curtains.

Not realizing he had moved forward, trying to get a clearer look at her, he collided with a small metal patio table. He tried to stop the table from toppling over, but to his horror he and the table continued to fall, landing on the cement patio. He cringed from the crashing sound of the metal hitting the cement, followed by Meg's piercing screams. He had to get out of there. It wasn't until he tried to stand up that he realized his pant leg had gotten caught on one of the table legs.

His eyes burned from the sweat running down his face as he struggled to free his pant leg. Just as he was able to tear the fabric and free his pant leg, the backyard lights came on and the back door flew open. He looked up to see James running toward him.

Adrenaline kicked in as he ran to the back fence. He easily scaled the fence, landing on the other side with a thud. He jumped up and continued running toward the back alley. He had just passed the side gate when the gate flew open. James ran out of the gate and continued chasing him. He was able to outrun James and escaped down the dark alley.

****

James was just dozing off when he heard a loud crash, followed by Meg's screams. James jumped up, grabbing his gun and flashlight from the nightstand. He almost ran into Meg in the hallway.

"Someone's in the backyard!" she yelled.

"You stay here!" yelled James

James, gun and flashlight in hand, ran to the back door. He needed light and the element of surprise. He turned the doorknob, unlocking the door and leaving it slightly ajar. In one swift move, he hit the light switch to the back lights and kicked the door open. He ran out just as the prowler ran toward the back fence. He was only able to see the back of the prowler with his flashlight, as the prowler scaled the back fence.

James ran to the back gate, secured by a bolt lock on the inside of the gate. He opened the gate just as the prowler ran past him. He chased him to the alley, but the guy was too fast and disappeared into the darkness.

It was at that moment James realized he was in his pajamas and barefoot. The alley was covered in small stones and broken glass, making it impossible for him to continue the chase without destroying the bottoms of his feet. Even if he'd been dressed for a foot chase, he doubted he would've been able to keep up with this guy.

The police spent the next two hours searching the alley and the surrounding area for the prowler, but he had managed to escape.

James, an FBI agent, had developed a strong relationship with the Monrovia PD and recognized the two officers at their front door.

They started laughing.

"Good to see you, James," said the officer. "Love the outfit."

"I always chase criminals in my pajamas and bare feet."

Any thoughts on who this guy might be?"

"Not a clue," said James.

He handed the officer a piece of blood-soaked fabric.

"Looks like he got tangled up on the leg of the table. I pulled this off one of the table legs. I was only able to get a quick look at him. He was tall with a slender build and wearing dark clothes. I'm getting way too old for foot chases."

The officer patted James on the shoulder.

"Sadly, age eventually catches up with all of us."

"Thanks, I feel much better."

"Just give us a call if you have any more problems. By the way, congratulations on your retirement."

"Thanks. If I get bored, can I still visit you guys?"

"You bet, come by anytime."

Meg put her arms around James and gave him a kiss.

"I'm going to keep him very busy. Just wait until he sees the list of chores waiting for him."

James groaned. "I was afraid of that."

They watched as the patrol car pulled away.

James held Meg in his arms. "Well, this has been quite a night. From now on I'm going to keep my shoes by the bed."

"Maybe it's time to get a watchdog," said Meg.

James smiled at Meg. "I guess this is a good excuse to go puppy shopping. Now let's go to bed. I doubt that he'll be back tonight."

****

He had managed to avoid the police. He watched from behind a thick hedge directly across the street from the Riley house. He felt something warm run down his lower leg from the deep gash on his leg. His stupidity had almost blown the whole plan. He couldn't afford to make stupid mistakes.

"Goodnight and sleep tight my friend, we will meet again."

Chapter 2

Friday, September 15, 1967
Los Angeles, California
FBI Office

It was a typical autumn day in Southern California. The Santa Ana winds had blown in and temperatures were in the nineties.

Assistant Special Agent James Riley looked out the window of his LA office for the last time. He was retiring after thirty years with the FBI.

James and his wife, Meg, had met in 1939, when they both worked at the FBI office in Washington, D.C. They were married in December of 1940. The summer after they married, James transferred to the LA field office so they could be closer to Meg's parents. They settled in Monrovia, a small town in the foothills of the San Gabriel Valley. Their daughter was born on October 31, 1941.

The war years from 1941 to 1945 brought many changes to the FBI. During those years, James was assigned to the Foreign Counter Intelligence Unit, investigating espionage cases.

After the war, he accepted a promotion to squad supervisor and transferred to the criminal unit. Over the years he had turned down several promotions because he loved being out in the field. This decision had been difficult for his family life, but he was one of the lucky ones. Meg, having worked in an FBI office, understood his job. She never complained and was the glue that held their family together.

In 1962, he accepted a promotion to assistant special agent in charge working directly under Special Agent in Charge Hank Welch.

James looked at his watch; it was almost five. He had promised Meg that he would be home by six. They had plans to go out to dinner with Meg's parents and their close friends, George and Elizabeth Johnson, to celebrate his retirement.

His daughter, Clair, and her husband, Tom, lived in Ohio. He had hoped they would be able to come out and help them celebrate, but they weren't able to get away from their jobs. He and Meg decided their first trip would be a car trip to Ohio to visit the kids.

James walked over to Hank's office. Hank Welch had been at their office for two years. He was in his early forties and looked just like Buddy Holly without the glasses.

"Well, Hank, I guess this is it," announced James.

James handed Hank his badge.

"I hate to admit it, but I'm going to miss this place."

"Are you sure you don't want to change your mind?"

"No way. Meg would kill me! I think you're going to be happy with Jack Richards. He's handled some tough cases and seems to have a good working relationship with his fellow agents."

"I agree, he's a good fit for this unit."

Hank walked over and shook James' hand. "I'm going to miss you, my friend. This place won't be the same without you. Now, get the hell out of here."

"I'll keep in touch."

"That's what they all say."

James went back to his office, grabbed the last box of his personal items, and headed for the elevator. Where had all the years gone? His dark hair had turned to silver and he had a lot more aches and pains. Meg, on the other hand, was still stunning. She was tall and slim with porcelain skin and red hair. He couldn't wait to see what the future held for them.

James took the elevator down to the parking garage and walked to his car. He opened the trunk and moved some things around to make room for the last box. Just as he started to put the last box in the trunk, he heard someone or something moving around the parking structure. He lowered the trunk lid. He didn't see anyone. Figuring it was just noise from the street, he shoved the last box into the trunk and closed it. That's when he saw someone standing near the elevator. Although the lighting was dim in the garage, he could make out a man. The man wore a baseball cap and he had pulled it down to cover his face.

"What are you doing down here? This is a private parking garage."

The man just stood there, not saying a word.

James' instincts kicked in and he loosened the snap on his holster.

Like other agents who retired before him, he had made the decision to get his private investigator license, which included a concealed-carry permit.

When James stepped toward him, the man spun around and started running out of the parking garage, James in pursuit. The man was fast and beat James to the street. Fortunately for the man, it was the end of the workday and the streets were crowded with people just getting off work and rushing to parking garages and bus stops. By the time James reached the street, the man had disappeared into the crowded city sidewalks.

James was walking back to his car when he heard the elevator door open and Hank walked out.

"James, what are you still doing here?"

"Some guy was standing by the elevator. I don't know where the guy came from; he wasn't there when I walked out of the elevator. I asked him what he was doing here, but he didn't respond. When I walked toward him, he ran out of the garage. I ran after him, but by the time I reached the street he was gone."

"Probably looking to break into cars," said Hank. "I'll report it to the building security."

"Maybe."

"Got something on your mind, James?"

"This is going to sound like a stretch. I think this could possibly be the same guy who was prowling around my house last month."

"What makes you think it's the same guy?"

"I know that I didn't see their faces, but both were tall with a slender build. However, that isn't what caught my attention. They both had a distinct stride when they ran, like a well-trained athlete."

"Are you thinking that you have a stalker?"

"I hope not," said James.

"Well, if you're being stalked, I'm glad you have your vicious watchdog to protect you."

"Very funny."

James had been the butt of many jokes when the guys in the office found out that his "vicious watchdog" was a six-pound, snow-white Maltese named Ginger. Her one and only aggressive asset was a high-pitched bark that could shatter a glass.

James looked at his watch. It was almost six. "I really need to get out of here."

James waved to Hank as he drove out of the garage.

He couldn't stop thinking about the man in the garage. He

tried to convince himself that he was being paranoid, but he couldn't let go of a gut feeling that he and his family were being watched.

****

The drive on the freeway from LA to Monrovia was about thirty minutes, depending on the traffic. It gave James time to gather his thoughts about leaving a job he loved. It was a difficult decision, but it was the right time. Of course, he did have his PI license. If he got bored he could always start his own PI business. However, this wasn't the time to share that idea with Meg.

James pulled into the driveway at six thirty. Coming home was always the best part of his day. They had purchased the 1914 Craftsman house in 1950. The front of the house had a large porch that overlooked a large yard of lush green grass and Meg's rose garden. Shade from a large pine tree helped cool the house on hot summer days. They had a large backyard that extended to the alley behind their house. Three years ago, they had put in a pool and large patio, from which they enjoyed a magnificent view of the San Gabriel Mountains.

Chapter 3

Thursday, September 14
Columbus, Ohio Airport

Clair wasn't a fan of flying. She grabbed Tom's hand as the plane moved down the runway and lifted into the air. She gave a sigh of relief as the plane leveled off and they were in cruise mode. They were finally on their way to California to celebrate her dad's retirement.

Tom leaned over and kissed Clair on the cheek. "I can't wait to see your dad's face when he sees us," he said.

"Me too. I'm amazed that my mom was able to keep this retirement party a secret from my dad."

"Do you think it's going to be difficult for your dad to adjust to civilian life?"

"I'm sure it will be, but I know my mom can get him through the transition."

"Wait until we tell them that we're moving back to California."

****

It was early evening when their plane landed at LAX. Meg's

parents, Don and Jane Smith, waited for Clair and Tom at the gate. They hadn't seen their granddaughter since her wedding two years ago.

"There they are!" yelled Jane.

Clair ran to her grandmother and gave her a huge hug.

Don put his arms out. "What about me?"

Clair ran into his arms.

Tom stood back, not sure what he should do. Tom's family was very reserved and hugs weren't the norm. He was amazed and envious that Clair's family was so comfortable showing affection for each other.

"Hey, Tom, get over here and give me a hug," Jane said.

Tom smiled. He walked over to Jane and gave her a hug and shook Don's hand.

"How was your trip?" asked Don.

"Once Clair let go of my hand, it was great," said Tom.

"Let's get your luggage and get out of here," said Don. "You can give your mom a call when we get back to the house."

Luggage in hand, they walked out the door of the airport and headed to the car. They hadn't noticed the man watching them.

As soon as the group was out of sight, the man used the pay phone.

"They're here," he said.

He hung up the phone and walked out of the airport.

Chapter 4

Friday, September 15

Bob Maywood sped down the 605 Freeway in his rental car, a 1967 Ford Shelby Mustang, black with gold strips. He had all the windows down so he could enjoy the warm evening. A far cry from the cold wet weather in Seattle.

He pulled off the freeway and drove through the streets of Monrovia. He turned on Encinitas and parked down the street from James' house. He couldn't wait to see his old friends. It had been too long.

Bob had retired as the US commissioner in Alaska in 1951. He moved to Seattle and started a new career, writing mystery novels based on his experiences in Alaska. He had a great life, traveling, meeting interesting people, especially beautiful women. However, there were times when he regretted not having a family.

He saw James pull into the driveway. As soon as James entered the house, Bob moved his car across the street from the house. After about ten minutes, he started to cross the street, then remembered he had left his wallet in the glove compartment. He was unlocking the car door when he heard rustling in the large hedge near his car. He stopped and listened.

He was startled by a loud cry. A black cat came running out of the bushes followed by a large gray cat. The gray cat took one look at Bob and ran away.

Bob hoped for a friendlier greeting at the party.

****

The hedge across the street from the Riley house had become his regular hiding place. James' daughter and son-in-law arrived with the older couple that had picked them up at the airport. He watched them unload their luggage from the trunk, confirming where they would be staying.

Once James was in the house, he started to climb out of the hedge. He stopped when the black Shelby parked in front of his hiding place. He thought it was safe to move when the driver started to walk across the street, but then the driver returned to the car.

Startled, he stepped back into the hedge, causing a rustling sound. The driver walked closer, staring into the hedge.

He held his breath; his heart was beating so hard it felt like it would explode.

It was at that moment that he heard the distinct howling of cats fighting. The two cats ran through the hedge, ran past the driver, and continued running down the street.

The driver shrugged his shoulders and walked away.

Now, he had never been a fan of cats, but those stupid cats had just saved his butt. He decided it was time to get out of there. He had all the info he needed for now.

Chapter 5

Friday, September 15

Meg checked the clock; it was almost six and James wasn't home yet. It wasn't like him to be late. James thought they were meeting family at a restaurant to celebrate his retirement. He had no idea that she had planned a huge surprise party.

The weather had cooperated, allowing for the party to be moved outside by the pool. George and Tom had put up lights around the pool, and set up an outside bar and tables for the food.

Clair walked over and gave her mom a hug. She was wearing the opal and diamond necklace that James and Meg had given her when she graduated from college.

"You're still wearing the necklace we gave you," said Meg.

"I never take it off," said Clair. "Mom, you look amazing."

Meg wore black bell-bottom dress pants and a white button-down shirt. Her thick red hair was pulled up in a French twist. Meg had perfect skin. The only makeup she needed was a little mascara and lipstick.

"Wait until Dad sees you in this outfit."

"Wait until your dad finds out how much I spent on this outfit!"

"I can't wait to see Dad's face when he sees us. Where is Uncle Bob?"

"He's going to wait until your dad gets here. Remember, don't tell Uncle George about Bob."

Bob and James met in 1939 when James was assigned to a multiple murder case in the Dutch Hills of Alaska. That was also where James met George Johnson. George's brother and sister-in-law were two of the murder victims. The three men established a strong bond working the case and bringing the perpetrators to justice.

Over the years, Bob and James had kept in touch by phone, but hadn't seen each other for several years.

George Johnson and his wife, Elizabeth, lived in Monrovia and were the reason that James and Meg moved to Monrovia. The two families were close friends.

George and Elizabeth walked over to Meg.

Meg and Elizabeth had been going crazy trying to keep Bob's visit a secret. They wanted the reunion to be a surprise for James and George. They couldn't wait to see the three of them together again.

"Where the hell is the guest of honor?" George asked.

"He should have been here by now. It's not like him to be late."

George put his arm around her. "Probably still saying his good-byes."

Meg was relieved when she heard his car pull into the driveway at six thirty. "Quiet everyone, he's here."

Meg met James at the door and gave him a big kiss. Before he could apologize for being late, the doors to the dining room opened and everyone yelled, "Surprise!"

James couldn't believe Meg had pulled this off. She was amazing. He was surprised and elated when he saw Clair and Tom standing next to Meg's parents. He gave Clair and Tom a hug.

"I thought you couldn't make it," he said.

"We wouldn't have missed this for the world," said Clair. "Grandma and Grandpa picked us up from the airport and let us stay at their house."

James hugged Jane and shook Don's hand. "Thank you for taking care of the kids," said James.

"It was our pleasure," said Jane.

George and Elizabeth walked over to James. George slapped him on the back. "Congratulations," said George. "Great party. Maybe I need to retire."

The doorbell rang.

"James, could you get the door?" Meg asked.

James thought it odd that she wanted him to answer the door; after all, he was the guest of honor. When he opened the door, he couldn't believe his eyes.

"Bob, you old fart, how the hell are you? Come on in and join the party. Hey, George, look who's here!"

George walked over and shook Bob's hand. "Damn, it's been a long time," George said. "You look good for an old fart."

James laughed. "Some things never change."

Hank walked up and shook hands with George and Bob.

"Hank, how the hell did you beat me home?" asked James.

"I didn't. I was behind you all the way home. I parked around the corner. Meg let me in the back. I finally get to meet the three musketeers who solved one of the biggest murder cases in Alaska. I've only heard the story like a hundred times!"

"Hank, where's your wife?"

"Tina wasn't feeling well. She sends her best."

"Sorry she couldn't make it," said James. "Hope she starts feeling better."

"I'm sure it's nothing serious. She didn't want me to miss the party."

****

It was one in the morning and most of the guests had left. Elizabeth and the kids helped Meg put away the food and clean up the kitchen.

Clair walked over to Meg. "Mom, if you don't mind, Tom and

I are going to call it a night."

"Of course, I don't mind. See you in the morning."

Meg turned to Elizabeth. "It's so hard having Clair so far away. When she decided to go Ohio State, I never dreamed that she would marry an Ohio boy and live in in Ohio. We do love Tom and I know that he takes good care of her."

Elizabeth gave Meg hug. "You never know what the future holds."

Meg and Elizabeth walked out to the pool, where Bob, James, and George were still in deep conversation.

They looked up when Meg and Elizabeth walked outside.

"You are two lucky SOBs," said Bob. "How did you manage to get these gorgeous women to marry you?"

Meg's face turned beet red.

"George, I hate to interrupt you, but we really need to go," said Elizabeth.

"You're right, we need to get up early. We're driving to Illinois. Elizabeth's family is having a big family reunion in Quincy. We'll be gone for four weeks."

"Is George Jr. going with you?" asked James.

"No," said George. "He decided to stay here and run the business while we're gone. He's ready for the responsibility."

"George, so glad that you and Elizabeth were able to make it," said James. "Have a safe trip."

Bob walked over to George. "George, it was great seeing you

again. If you're ever in Seattle, look me up. I know some great restaurants."

"You bet," said George.

They walked George and Elizabeth to their car. Bob followed them out, so he could get his bags from the car.

George and James walked with Bob to the Shelby.

"Great ride," said James. "You must be selling a lot of books!"

"I wish. Sorry to disappoint, but this car belongs to Hertz."

"It will happen, my friend."

When they came in, Meg said her goodnights.

"Bob, the guest room is ready. James can show you the way."

"Thanks."

By the time James climbed into bed, Meg was sound asleep with Ginger snuggled next to her. He kissed her on the cheek. Exhausted, he fell into a deep sleep.

Chapter 6

Saturday, September 16

James woke up to the smell of freshly brewed coffee and bacon frying. He could hear Meg and Clair chatting in the kitchen. It was so good to have her home, even if it was just for a few days. She had grown up so fast. He couldn't believe that she was married and teaching first-graders. It didn't seem that long ago that Clair was in first grade.

James took a quick shower and made it to the kitchen just in time for breakfast. Bob was sitting at the table enjoying a cup of coffee.

"Well, look who's up. How does it feel to be retired?"

"I'm not sure," said James. "I guess it'll sink in on Monday morning when I don't have to get on the congested freeway."

Ginger was sitting under the table, probably hoping that someone would drop a crumb or two on the floor. When she saw James, she stood on her back legs and danced in circles. He reached down and picked her up. She immediately relaxed in his arms.

"She's been a pain this morning," said Meg. "Apparently we're being punished for making her stay in our bedroom during the party."

Ginger started squirming, so James put her down. She went over and curled up in her bed.

"Now that everyone is here, I need your attention," Clair said. "We have a surprise! We're moving back to California. Tom has accepted an accounting position with a firm in Pasadena. I've been offered a teaching position at Monroe Elementary. Tom starts his job in January. I'm going to start substituting after the Christmas break. I'll start teaching full time in September."

Tears of joy welled up in Meg's eyes.

"That's not good news, it's great news!" James exclaimed.

"We're hoping to find a house in this neighborhood," said Clair. "Tom has never had a chance to see the neighborhood, so I thought I would take him on a tour. We'll be back in time for lunch and a swim."

Chapter 7

Saturday, September 16

The van, with "Smith's House Painting" written on the side, pulled into the neighborhood and parked down the street from the Riley house. Two men, wearing white overhauls, got out of the van and put up the hood. They started banging around the engine, making it look like they were having car trouble.

Virgil Potter and Red McCoy had been cellmates in the LA County jail. They were small-time crooks whose crimes consisted of burglary and car thefts. They decided to work together after their release. Kidnapping was a new gig for them and promised a big payday.

They had watched and waited for the opportunity to get her alone. They knew that they were staying with her parents, but they hadn't been able to get near her and were running out of time. But their luck was about to change.

They watched as Clair and her husband walked out of the house and started walking down the street.

"She's still not alone," said Red.

"This might be our only chance," said Virgil. "We'll just have to take both of them."

They closed the hood and jumped into the van. They waited until the couple disappeared around the corner. They drove slowly down the street, following the couple through the neighborhood.

Chapter 8

Saturday, September 16

Clair and Tom decided to walk down one more block before starting back to her parents' house. The street was lined with beautiful old homes and manicured lawns. Except for one house, an old Victorian home that sat on a large lot at the end of the street. Overgrown weeds, bushes, and trees obscured the front of the house.

"I haven't seen that house in years," said Clair. "We used to call it the haunted house."

"I bet it was a beautiful house at one time. Do you know who lived there?" Tom asked.

"Two sisters lived there," said Clair. "They never married. They passed away several years ago. The house has been vacant for a long time. I wonder if the family still owns the house. It would be weird for someone to buy it and not take care of it. I'm surprised that the city hasn't gone after the owner."

"I bet we could get it real cheap," said Tom.

Clair furrowed her brow. "It would cost a fortune to restore that house. It probably needs all new wiring and plumbing. Not to mention all the dry rot and termite damage."

"It does need work," said Tom. "I like the idea of restoring it. Remember, I worked in construction to pay for school. Maybe now that your dad is retired, he would be willing to help."

"My dad is pretty handy," said Clair. "Not sure he would want to take on such a large project."

Still intrigued with the house, Tom grabbed Clair's hand. "Let's go see if the door is unlocked."

Clair glared at Tom. "Are you crazy, we could get in trouble for trespassing!"

"No one's going to know. Just a quick look and then we'll leave. I promise."

Clair checked her watch. "Okay, just a quick look."

They climbed the steps to the porch. The wood on the steps and porch cracked and snapped under their feet. Clair was surprised and relieved the porch didn't collapse. The front door was huge, with three beveled glass windows at the top of the door. Tom turned the doorknob. To his surprise, the door opened. Tom stood there with a huge grin on his face.

"We're not breaking in if the door isn't locked!"

"Great, you can explain that to the cops when they arrest us for trespassing!"

Tom laughed. "I'm sure your dad would bail us out."

"He would bail me out, but I'm not so sure about you," she teased.

Tom grabbed her hand and they entered the house. It was dark and it took a minute for their eyes to adjust.

"This must be the living room," said Clair.

The only furniture in the room was a broken chair. Thick dust covered the floor.

"Doesn't look like anyone has been in the house in years," said Tom.

Clair held on to Tom's arm. "Tom, I'm scared."

"Scared of what?" Tom teased. "The boogeyman!"

They heard the floorboards creak on the staircase.

"What was that?" cried Clair.

They both jumped when a big gray cat ran down the stairs. The cat took one look at them and ran back up the stairs. Relieved, they continued to explore the downstairs. The kitchen was at the back of the house. There was a formal dining room and a library.

"Since we're here, we might as well take a look upstairs," said Tom.

"Just a quick look. We need to get back for lunch."

They climbed the stairs to the second floor. There were five small bedrooms and a bathroom. All the bedrooms had fireplaces.

"Wow, this place must have been amazing," said Tom.

"I have to admit, it's an incredible house."

They heard rustling coming from one of the bedrooms at the end of the hallway.

"Must be the cat," said Clair.

Clair and Tom walked down to the end of the hallway and entered the bedroom. The cat was curled up in the corner nursing her kittens. They were so focused on the cats, they didn't see the two men sneaking up behind them.

****

They couldn't believe their luck. They were able to park the van at the back of the property, where it was well hidden by the overgrown trees. They filled a bag with their "kidnapping kit," rags, chloroform, rope, and duct tape.

They watched the couple from a side window. When the couple went upstairs, they entered through the front door and followed them. They had planned to jump them on the stairs, but decided to wait. It was a good decision. When the young couple went into one of the bedrooms, they moved in. It was over in a matter of minutes. They carried them out the back of the house and put them in the van. They hadn't noticed Clair's necklace on the floor.

Chapter 9

Saturday, September 16

It was three and Clair and Tom hadn't returned from their walk. Meg walked out to the pool, where James and Bob were relaxing.

"James, I'm worried. The kids were supposed to be back by two."

"They probably just lost track of time. I'm sure they will be home soon. They're old enough to take care of themselves. They couldn't be in a safer neighborhood."

"I guess you're right," said Meg.

****

It was five and Clair and Tom still hadn't returned. It would be dark soon. Now James was getting concerned.

"Meg, Bob and I are going to drive around the neighborhood and look for them. I need you to stay here in case they show up."

James drove through the entire neighborhood, but Clair and Tom were nowhere to be found. They stopped and talked to several of the neighbors, who told them they had seen them walking down the street. However, no one remembered seeing them come back.

They saw a man working in his front yard

"We haven't talked to that man," said Bob.

"Excuse me, sir. My name is James Riley and this is my friend Bob Maywood. I live over on Encinitas. I'm looking for my daughter and son-in-law. They went for a walk early this afternoon and didn't return. My daughter is a tall redhead."

"They walked past our house early this afternoon," said the man. "They were looking at the old abandoned house at the end of our street. That house is in bad condition. Maybe they went exploring and had an accident."

"Thanks."

James and Bob jumped in the car and drove down to the old house. James tried the front door and it was open. He leaned in and called out their names, but no one answered. It was getting dark.

"Bob, I have a couple of flashlights in the car. I'll be right back."

A few minutes later James returned with the flashlights.

They stood at the front door and shined the flashlights on the floor. The living room floor was covered in a blanket of thick dust. Fresh footprints covered the floor.

It looked like there were footprints from at least three different people. They needed to check the rest of the first floor.

Being careful not to disturb the footprints, they searched the downstairs. Once they left the living room, the footprints appeared to be from just two people.

They returned to the stairs to the second floor.

"Hey, James, there are more footprints that match the one in the living room."

The footprints went up the stairs and down the hallway. It appeared that all of the bedrooms were on the second floor. They continued down the hallway searching each bedroom. The only room left was at the end of the hallway. James entered the bedroom and saw something on the floor. As he approached the item he realized it was a rag. He could smell the chloroform. Next to the chloroform-soaked rag was a necklace.

When Bob entered the bedroom, he saw James staring at the floor. "Did you find something?"

"Yes, an opal and diamond necklace. We gave it to Clair when she graduated from college. Opal is Clair's birthstone. She never took it off."

Chapter 10

Saturday, September 16

Bob ran to the house next door and called the police. Within minutes the police were all over the crime scene. They blocked off the street and canvassed all the surrounding streets. The police chief pulled up. He and James had collaborated on several cases over the years and had developed a great working relationship.

"We are contacting the FBI and I requested Special Agent in Charge Hank Welch. I figured you would want the best."

"Chief, I have one more request. A couple of reporters are out front. We need to keep this quiet. If the news media gets wind of this, the kidnappers might panic and kill them."

"I agree. Let me take care of this."

The chief walked over to the reporters. A few minutes later he returned.

"Told them that it was a false alarm and that the couple came home on their own. Explained that we are just making sure the house is secure and are planning to contact the owners since this house is an accident waiting to happen."

"Thanks, that works for me."

Bob stayed at the scene while James went back to the house. James wanted to be the one to break the news to Meg.

****

When James walked into the house, Meg was sitting on the couch next to the phone.

"James, what's going on?"

James sat down and held her hands. "I'm not going to sugarcoat this. It looks like Clair and Tom were abducted. They were seen going into that old abandoned house two streets over, but no one saw them come out. Bob and I found evidence of a struggle in one of the upstairs bedrooms. Meg, we found Clair's necklace next to a cloth soaked in chloroform."

The color drained from Meg's face. Tears ran down her cheeks. "Clair loved that necklace. She would never take it off," Meg cried. "I just want my baby back."

"We're going to find them. The FBI's taking over the investigation and I've requested that Hank take the lead. We didn't find any blood at the house. That's a good sign that they were alive when they left the house."

"Do you think this is a case of them being in the wrong place at the wrong time?"

"It could have been a crime of opportunity, but we need to be prepared in case we get a ransom demand."

Meg dried her eyes. She was determined to keep calm; this wasn't the time for self-pity.

"We've sent out alerts to all law enforcement agencies. We will find them."

"Is this going to be on the news?" she asked.

"Not if we can help it."

He told her about the story the Monrovia PD chief gave the news media.

"Don't you think I should call my parents and Tom's parents? What if there is a leak to the news media?"

"It's a risk we have to take. Until we figure out what we're dealing with, the fewer people that know the better. Meg, we're going to find Clair and Tom and bring them home."

Meg buried her face in his shoulder and started sobbing. James had never seen her like this.

"I told myself I wasn't going to cry," she said. "I am so scared. I can't understand why anyone would want to harm Clair and Tom."

James cradled her in his arms.

****

Hank arrived at their house a few minutes later accompanied by a team of agents. They went to work setting up the phone-tapping equipment.

They moved to the kitchen so the agents could get everything set up.

"Meg, I forgot to tell you why I was running so late on Friday night," said James. "I had an encounter with some guy in the parking garage at work. When I tried to approach him, he ran out of the garage. I chased him, but he got away. Hank figured he was probably there to break into cars, but now I'm not so sure!"

"Who do you think it is?" asked Meg

"I think our prowler and the guy I encountered in the parking structure could be the same person."

"What prowler?" asked Bob.

"Last month, I chased a guy who was sneaking around our house."

"How can you be so sure it's the same guy?" asked Bob.

"I can't be totally sure. They both have the same physical appearance and both are athletic."

"If this is the same guy, who is he and why would he kidnap Clair and Tom?" asked Bob.

"I don't know, but I don't think he's working alone. It would have taken more than one person to take down Clair and Tom."

"That would be consistent with all the footprints at the house," Hank added.

"We haven't received a ransom request," said James. "Even if they did want money, we aren't rich people."

"What if the motive is revenge and not money?" asked Bob.

"I've been thinking the same thing," said James. "I've made a lot of enemies over the years."

****

James walked Hank to his car.

"James, until we receive a ransom demand, it makes sense to investigate the revenge angle. We need to review your cases. I can put three or four of my best guys on this tonight. If you are right about the prowler and the guy in the garage being the same person, he is probably watching our every move. There will be two agents posted outside your house until this nightmare is over."

"Hank, we can't waste any time. Clair and Tom's lives are on the line! Let me work with you to find my daughter. Remember, I have my PI license and I can legally carry a gun!"

"James, we're dealing with someone targeting you and your family! You and Meg could be their next target. You need to stay with Meg. I promise to call you if we get any leads."

"Hank, I know you're right. It's just so hard to step back and take on the roles of a civilian and victim. I guess retirement is going to be more of an adjustment then I anticipated."

Chapter 11

Saturday, September 16

It was a two-hour drive to the cabin. The cabin was several feet from the dirt road, hidden by large pine trees. The windows had been boarded up and the door was secured with a padlock.

Virgil pulled a key from his pocket and unlocked the padlock. The cabin was small. The main room of the cabin had a living room, fireplace, and a small kitchen with a wood-burning stove. There was a separate bedroom and bathroom.

They carried the couple, still out cold, into the bedroom and laid them on the bed. Virgil checked to make sure the ropes binding their hands and feet were secure.

Virgil returned to the main room. "Man, this place is a real dump. There isn't even a door on the bedroom."

"What did you expect, a fancy hotel?"

Virgil grumbled something under his breath and started rummaging through the kitchen. "Shit, Red, there's nothing to eat or drink in this dump. Why don't we go to town and get some chow?"

"Don't be stupid," said Red. "The boss is going to be pissed when he finds out we took both of them. We leave and they get away we're dead."

"The boss ain't gonna get mad. Two victims mean more money. Anyway, they're so knocked out from the chloroform they won't wake up for hours.," said Virgil. "Even if they do wake up, they ain't goin' nowhere. Hey, if it makes you feel better we can get some food for our guests. The boss ain't gonna find out!"

Red was reluctant, but finally agreed. "We go to town, get the food, and come back!"

"Sure, Red, that's what we're gonna do. You worry too much."

As much as he wanted to believe Virgil, he knew they were making a big mistake.

They secured the cabin and headed to town.

Chapter 12

Sunday September 17
6:00 AM

Red was startled out of a deep sleep by the thud of a large pinecone landing on the top of the van. The early-morning sunshine shone brightly through the thin fabric curtains that covered the windows of the van. It took a few minutes for him to clear his head. Fear raged through his body when he realized they had really screwed up.

"Wake up!"

Virgil rolled over and moaned. "What the hell happened?"

"We got drunk and passed out, that's what happened. Damn, Virgil, we are in deep shit. You better hope that they didn't get away!"

"Chill out. There's no way they could get away. Hell, we gave them enough chloroform to knock them out for hours. Even if they did wake up, they're tied up and there's no one around to hear them yell for help."

"I hope you're right," said Red. "We better get back to the cabin."

Virgil sped out of the parking lot, recklessly navigating the van up the winding mountain road.

"Slow down, Virgil!" yelled Red. "We don't need the cops pulling us over."

Virgil smiled, exposing his missing teeth. "Geez, Red, you whine like a little girl."

The van started to shake violently. Virgil looked in the side-view mirror just as the left rear tire broke loose and bounced across the road. Sparks flew and the smell of hot metal and asphalt permeated the van. The van swerved. Virgil fought to keep control, but it was too late. The van flipped and rolled down the side of the mountain, landing upside down. A large tree stopped it from plummeting down the steep hill.

Red opened his eyes. He had a massive headache and blood was running down the side of his face. The last thing he remembered was the van flipping over. He'd been thrown from the van and had landed in a clearing just a few feet from the van. He couldn't believe that he was still alive. He saw Virgil lying next to a large boulder.

"Virgil, are you okay?"

Virgil didn't answer.

Red crawled over to Virgil and let out a gasp. Virgil was unrecognizable. His skull had been crushed when he landed on the boulder.

"Damn, Virgil, I told you to slow down!"

Red heard footsteps. He looked up and saw a man walking toward him. He let out a sigh of relief.

"Man, am I glad to see you. Virgil's dead and I'm hurt real bad!"

The man just stood there with a malicious smile on his face. He didn't utter a word.

Red's mouth was dry and sweat poured down his face. "It was Virgil's idea. I swear I tried to stop him, but you know how he was. We were on our way back to the cabin."

The man pulled out a gun. "You idiot. I never planned on keeping you around. You and Virgil were supposed to die in the crash."

Red didn't move, paralyzed by fear.

"You idiots should have known that I had people watching you."

Red knew what was coming. He rolled over on his stomach and closed his eyes. It was over in a second.

Hiring Red and Virgil had been a mistake. How could he have been so stupid? The ground was covered with all the stuff from the van. He needed to remove anything that could link the van to the kidnapping. He hadn't anticipated Red surviving the crash. Now he had to get rid of Red's body, since it would be obvious he wasn't an accident victim. All he had to do was throw the body over the side of the hill. Unfortunately, his plans were interrupted by voices coming from the road above the crash scene. He didn't have a choice. He hurried down the trail to a clearing where he had left his truck.

Chapter 13

Sunday, September 17

Sunlight streamed through the gaps in the boards that covered the windows. Clair opened her eyes. She was lying on a bed, her hands and feet bound with rope. The pain from the ropes rubbing against her fair skin was intense. She could feel someone breathing on the back of her neck. She prayed that it was Tom.

It was a struggle, but she finally managed to roll over. She was relieved to see Tom.

"Tom, wake up!"

Tom groaned and opened his eyes.

"Tom, be quiet. There might be someone sitting outside this room."

They continued in lowered voices.

"Are you okay?"

"Oh, I'm just great. My head is throbbing, the rope is digging into my skin, and I think I'm going to vomit!"

"Well if you're are going to throw up, could you please roll over?"

Clair scowled at him.

She took an inventory of the room. There wasn't a bedroom door. An old sheet covered the doorway. The only furniture in the room was the bed and a small night table. There was a small bathroom, reminding her that she really had to pee. It appeared to be an old log cabin and she could smell the strong scent of pine.

"I'm so sorry I insisted on going into that house," said Tom. "I love you and I would never intentionally put you in danger."

"I love you too."

Tom struggled with the rope until he freed his hands. He moved quickly, untying the rope around his ankles and then freeing Clair. As soon as Clair was free she ran to the bathroom.

"Wait," whispered Tom.

He pulled the sheet, which covered the doorway, open just enough to see into the other room. To his relief, no one was there.

While Clair used the bathroom, Tom pulled down the sheet and entered the main room of the cabin. The cabin was small. There was one common area with a fireplace and a small kitchen. No refrigerator. When Clair came out of the bathroom she searched through the cabinets, but there wasn't any food. They had gone several hours without food or water and her stomach growled. She found a couple of glasses and filled them with water. It wasn't much, but it was refreshing.

"Tom, what time is it?"

"I don't know; my watch is gone."

Out of habit, Clair reached up to check for her necklace. "Oh no! My necklace is gone," she cried.

"I'm sorry, I know how much that necklace meant to you."

"Let's hope it fell off at the house. It would be evidence that we were there."

"I doubt that anyone's going to look for us at that house."

Clair's heart sank. "You're probably right."

The windows were boarded up and the door had been locked from the outside. The front door was heavy, so kicking it open wasn't an option. They decided the easiest and safest way was to climb out the bedroom window. They searched through the cabin for something to remove the boards from the window. Tom saw a pile of wood next to the old wood-burning stove. He dug through the woodpile and pulled out an ax.

Clair came out of the bedroom, proudly holding a slingshot. "Look what I found!"

"What are you going to do with a slingshot?"

"Hey, I'm the daughter of an FBI agent. I was taught to be resourceful and I'm a good shot."

"Why am I not surprised?"

Clair rummaged through the kitchen cabinets one more time and found a canteen. "Tom, this canteen looks like it's never been used."

She rinsed out the canteen and filled it with water.

Tom used the ax to break the window and remove the boards. He used the handle of the ax to remove most of the glass. He pulled the blanket from the bed and used it to cover the broken glass on the bottom of the window. Tom went out the window first and looked around. When it was safe he helped Clair climb out.

It was early morning and the cool fresh air felt good.

"Wait a minute," said Clair. "I know where we are! We're in Big Bear. My grandparents have a vacation cabin up here."

"How can you be sure?"

"My grandparents built their cabin when I was five. We came up here all the time until I went away to college. We used to go hiking and horseback riding all through the area."

"Do they have a phone?"

"No. But at least we'll have shelter."

"Maybe we can find a cabin with a phone," said Tom.

"I don't think that's a good idea. We might be getting ourselves in a bigger mess. I think we better stay off the trails."

Tom gave her a hug. "Good idea. Lead the way, boss."

Tom was dressed in jeans and a T-shirt and sneakers. Clair was in shorts, a short-sleeve blouse, and sneakers. Neither one had a jacket. It was going to take two to three hours to get to the cabin. The temperatures would start dropping by late afternoon and they weren't dressed for a hike in the mountains. However, the good thing was that this cold was mild compared to the freezing Ohio winters.

"Tom, we better get going while we still have daylight."

Armed with an ax and a slingshot, they started walking. Clair grabbed some small rocks and put them in her pocket.

Chapter 14

Sunday, September 17

It was late afternoon when they finally arrived at the cabin. There was already a chill in the air.

Clair hadn't been there in years. Hopefully, they still kept a spare house key under the large potted plant on the porch.

"Tom, can you help me?"

Tom lifted the pot and Clair pulled out the key.

They decided to walk around the cabin to check for any signs of a break-in. They made their way around the cabin. Everything looked secure.

"Clair, what if someone else found the key and is waiting for us in the cabin?"

She reached in her pocket and grabbed a large stone.

Tom could hardly keep from laughing. "Wow, a David and Goliath moment."

Clair furrowed her brow. "Got a better idea?"

"Nope."

Tom slowly turned the key and opened the door.

She couldn't believe that nothing had changed. She had loved coming here as a child.

They searched the entire cabin and didn't find any signs that anyone had been there.

They were going to have to hike to the main highway and walk to town. However, it would be too dangerous for them to hike down to the road in the dark. They would have to wait until morning.

"I just hope the kidnappers don't know about this cabin," said Clair. "I also don't believe in coincidences. We were kidnapped in my parents' neighborhood and left in a cabin in Big Bear near my grandparents' cabin. There's a possibility that whoever was behind our kidnapping knows our family. Maybe we were supposed to escape and we're being watched. I just don't know why."

"The one thing that doesn't fit is the old house," said Tom. No one, including us, knew that we would be in that house. In fact, our walk was a last-minute decision."

"The only explanation is that they watched and waited for the opportunity to grab us. They must have been watching the house."

That possibility sent chills up her spine.

"We better not start a fire," said Clair. "We don't want to attract attention."

Clair found a flashlight and some blankets in the bedroom.

The cabinets in the kitchen were fully stocked with canned goods. She found a can of spam and some canned vegetables that didn't need to be heated up. She was dying for a cup of coffee, but water would have to do.

"Hope you like cold spam with cold vegetables and water!" said Clair.

"I'm so hungry I'll eat anything," Tom said.

They shoveled down their food and snuggled up under the blankets on the couch. They kept the ax and slingshot next to them. Exhausted, they dozed off.

The squeak of the doorknob woke them up.

Tom grabbed the ax and peeked out the window, but it was too dark to see who was on the porch. Headlights from a car coming up the dirt road sent the dark figure scurrying off the porch and disappearing into the darkness.

Clair's heart was pounding so loud she could hardly breathe.

"What if it's the kidnappers?" Clair whispered.

They watched as the car turned around and drove back down the dirt road.

"Maybe it was someone trying to find a cabin and got lost," said Tom.

Tom put his arms around Clair. "It's going to be alright," he said.

"Whoever was trying to get into the cabin is still out there," Clair cried. "What if he comes back?"

"As soon as it starts to get light, we're out of here," said Tom. "Until then, we need to secure the cabin."

They moved furniture in front of the door, and made sure that all the windows were locked.

Chapter 15

Sunday, September 17

It had been a long night of tossing and turning. Meg rolled over and looked at the clock, it was four thirty.

James and Bob had spent the night in the living room with the two agents, monitoring the phones. Meg got dressed and walked down the hallway to the living room. They all looked up when she walked into the room.

"Have you guys been up all night?" she asked.

"None of us could sleep," James said. "How about you?"

"I won't be able to sleep until I know that Clair and Tom are safe," she said. "I don't know about you guys, but I need some strong coffee. How about some breakfast?"

"Sounds good," said James. "We can't help the kids if we don't take care of ourselves."

****

They had just finished eating when the phone rang. It was Hank. "James, I hope I didn't wake you."

"We've been up for hours, couldn't sleep."

~ 53 ~

"My guys have been going through your old cases. I've flagged some cases I want you to look at. Is it okay if I come over?"

"Sure. We might even have some food and coffee for you!"

"Sounds good. I'll be there in thirty minutes."

****

When Hank arrived, they sat down at the kitchen table to review and discuss the cases.

Hank decided to include the file for the 1939 murder case in Alaska. Although he doubted the case had anything to do with the attacks on James' family, he didn't see any harm in revisiting the case.

"It doesn't make sense that someone would wait this long to get revenge," said James. "Usually, a person set on revenge will choose a significant date to carry out their revenge. Why twenty-eight years and not thirty years?"

"I would guess that most of the friends and close relatives of the murder suspects are dead or too old to care," said Bob.

Hank shook his head in agreement. "I agree, I don't think that case has anything to do with the abduction of Clair and Tom. But just to make sure, I'll have my agents check out the suspects' families and friends."

James shook hands with Hank. "Thanks for your help."

"No problem. I'll call if I find out anything."

Just as Hank was leaving the phone rang.

James waited for the agent to give him the thumbs-up and answered the phone. It wasn't the kidnappers.

"Hank, it's for you."

Hank took the phone and motioned James to listen on the other phone.

"This is Sgt. Jack Clark from the San Bernardino Sheriff's office. Your office gave me this number."

"No problem, how can I help you?"

"I think I have some evidence connected to your abduction case. There's been an accident up here involving an old van. The van lost a back tire and went off the road about a mile outside of Big Bear City. Both men were ejected. One guy landed on a large boulder, crushing his skull. The other guy had a broken arm and a mangled leg, but that's not what killed him. Someone shot him in the back of the head at close range. The impact from the crash blew the back doors open on the van, spreading the contents all over the side of the hill. We found rags, chloroform, and rope."

"Are you sure there wasn't anyone else in the van?" asked Hank.

"We're sure," answered the officer. "I thought you would want to see the crash scene. I left some officers to guard the sight."

"We're on our way," said Hank.

"Go to the San Bernardino office," Sgt. Clark explained. "I'll meet you there and drive you to the accident scene."

"If these guys were involved in Clair and Tom's abduction, where are the kids?" asked James. "There must be more people involved and we could still get a call. Meg, I need you and Bob to stay here in case there's a call. I'm going with Hank!"

Hank didn't argue with James.

Meg was obviously upset being left behind, but she agreed that she needed to stay by the phone.

James gave Meg a hug and a kiss. "I promise I'll call you."

"You better or you're in deep trouble," she scolded.

Chapter 16

Sunday, September 17

It was early Sunday afternoon when they arrived at the crash site. Hank and James made their way down the hill to the van. A large tree had stopped the van from falling all the way down the steep incline. According to the officers, there were two men in the van. It appeared that they were heading up the hill at a high rate when they lost a tire, causing the driver to lose control of the van.

The bodies hadn't been moved. The man by the boulder appeared to have died instantly from a crushed skull. The other man was on the ground near the other victim. He had suffered a gunshot wound to the back of the head. You could see drag marks that went from the van to where he now laid, indicating that he had survived the crash.

When they had finished clearing the crash scene, the coroner removed the bodies. The van was towed to the sheriff's garage.

They returned to the Sheriff's Office in Big Bear to go over the evidence.

"One of my officers asked around Big Bear City. The bartender at the local bar remembered the two men. The two men spent several hours at the bar. He said they could hardly walk when they left the bar. He had one of his friends at the bar follow them to make sure that they didn't try to drive. The friend said they staggered to an old van parked behind the bar. He watched them climb into the back of the van. He waited a few minutes and walked over to the van. He couldn't see in the windows, but he could hear snoring. The bartender was going to alert the sheriff, but decided that as long as they weren't causing any trouble he wasn't going to get involved. Early the next morning, they were seen speeding out of town."

"We know that they were heading up the hill, so where were they going?" asked James.

Sgt. Clark picked up the phone and made a call.

"We have a lot of unoccupied and abandoned cabins in this area. Your daughter and her husband are probably being held at one of those cabins. I have a friend who's a real estate agent. He handles most of the cabin sales and rentals in the area. I gave him a call and he gave me the location of the cabins that we need to search. I'm guessing that these idiots didn't leave them food or water. They could also be injured and need medical help."

****

They decided they could cover more territory if they split into two teams, James went with Sgt. Clark. Hank rode with Clark's partner, Officer Evans.

Clark's four-wheel drive moved easily up the dirt road. They had checked out several cabins but hadn't found any sign of Clair and Tom.

Clark stopped as soon as he saw the cabin. "I have a good feeling about this cabin." He grabbed his flashlight and wireless radio. "We need to walk the rest of the way."

The cabin was in bad shape. All the windows were boarded up and there was a padlock on the door. The cabin was dark and there wasn't any sign of life.

James walked around to the back of the cabin. "Hey, Clark, look at this!"

They found an open window. Broken glass and splintered boards covered the ground under the window. A blanket covered the windowsill. It was obvious that someone had escaped through the window. James prayed that it was Clair and Tom.

They broke the lock on the door and entered the cabin.

Clark went into the bedroom.

"James, look at this."

They found ropes on the floor by the bed. They found chloroform-soaked rags in the trash.

One thing that they didn't find was blood, giving them hope that the kids were still alive. Clark called Evans on the radio and told him what they had found at the cabin. Evans called the dispatcher and requested a forensic team to process the cabin.

****

James and Clark were standing outside of the cabin when Evans and Hank pulled up.

Hank walked over to James and patted him on the shoulder. "Don't worry, James, we're going to find them."

"I just hope it's not too late," said James. "I will never forgive myself if anything happens to Clair and Tom. I was an FBI agent for thirty years and I can't even protect my own daughter! I need to call Meg and let her know what's going on."

"I can stay with Clark," said Hank. "Evans, can drive you back to the office so you can call Meg? There's nothing more you can do here."

"You're right," said James.

****

Meg was startled when the phone rang. The FBI agent gave her the signal and they answered the phones. She was relieved when she heard James' voice. James told her what had happened so far.

"James, I think I know where the kids might be," Meg blurted out. "My parents' cabin!"

"Oh my God!" yelled James. "How could I be so stupid? Meg, I'll give you a call as soon as I can."

"Be careful, James. I love you."

James hung up the phone.

Officer Evans was waiting outside by the truck.

James ran out to the truck. "Evans, I think I know where the kids might be! My in-laws have a cabin a few miles from the abandoned cabin."

Evans radioed Clark and gave him the info.

"I just received an alert," said Clark. "Some guy drove by a cabin and saw a man messing with the front door. The headlights from the guy's car scared him off."

They decided to meet down the road from the cabin. That way they could hike to the cabin without being seen.

Chapter 17

Sunday, September 17

Clair and Tom, armed with a flashlight, ax, and slingshot, snuggled under the blankets.

Tom kissed Clair.

"Tom, I don't think this is a great time for romance."

"Hey, can't a guy just give his wife a kiss without ulterior motives? Anyway, I'm way too tired, so you're safe."

Clair giggled and snuggled even closer to him.

"Clair, why don't you try to get some sleep?"

She closed her eyes and immediately fell into a deep sleep.

Tom started to doze off when he heard someone trying to open the door.

"Clair, wake up, someone's outside."

Tom looked out the window, but it was too dark to see anything.

"What if it's the kidnappers?" she cried.

Tom grabbed the ax and flashlight and they hid behind the sofa.

"Clair, do you have the slingshot?"

"Yes, but I only have one small rock!"

"Okay, this is the plan. When they break through the door, I shine the flashlight on them and you take a shot at them. It might give us enough time to get away."

Clair gave Tom a kiss on the cheek. She put the stone in the slingshot.

"I'm ready!"

The door crashed open. Tom shone the flashlight at the man coming through the door. Clair aimed the slingshot at the man. The stone flew across the room, but it missed the man. Tom ran across the room and tackled him.

Suddenly the lights came on in the cabin and stopped the chaos. Tom was horrified when he realized he was sitting on his father-in-law. Tom stood up and helped James to his feet.

Clair ran to her dad. "Dad, are you okay? We thought you were the kidnappers. Someone tried to get in, but a car scared them off."

"I'm fine," said James. "What the hell flew past my head?"

Clair held up the slingshot. "Good thing I missed. How did you find us?"

"It's a long story. Your mom was sure that you were here."

"Do you remember anything about the kidnappers?" asked James.

"We never saw them," explained Tom. "They jumped us from

behind at the house. We woke up in an old cabin and they were gone."

"The kidnappers are dead. The sheriff found the bodies near their van outside of Big Bear City. Evidence found at the crash site leads us to the conclusion that they were the kidnappers. One of the men died in the crash. We're concerned because the other man survived the crash, but someone shot him in the head. There must be more people involved. You and Tom may still be in danger."

Tears welled up in Clair's eyes. Tom put his arms around Clair.

"I don't understand why anyone would want to hurt us!"

"I think we better get out of here," said Hank.

Chapter 18

Sunday, September 17

Meg jumped when the phone rang. She waited for the signal and answered the phone. She was relieved to hear James' voice.

"Someone wants to talk to you," he said.

"Hi, Mom!"

"Clair, is that you?"

"Yes, it's me!"

"Thank God you are you okay! Is Tom with you?"

"Yes, Mom, we're both okay and we love you!"

"I love you too, Clair. Let me talk to your dad."

"Meg, you were right, they were at the cabin," said James. "We're feeding them and getting their statements. I'll let you know when we are on our way home. Meg, I'm sure there were more people involved. Hank's requesting additional agents to watch the house. I love you and we'll be home soon."

"Please stay safe," Meg cried. "I love you too!"

Sgt. Clark called James and Hank into his office. "I just got the report from our mechanics on the van. The crash wasn't an accident. Someone loosened the lug nuts on the back, left tire. Whoever sabotaged the van didn't plan on anyone surviving the crash. It must have been a shock when he found one of them alive.

"We also have an ID on the two guys in the van. Red McCoy and Virgil Potter, small-time crooks who recently did time for burglary. They have quite an extensive criminal history but nothing violent. I doubt they were smart enough to pull off a kidnapping without help. I'm sure our shooter hadn't planned on shooting Red. It was his first mistake."

Chapter 19

Sunday, September 17

Meg hung up the phone. Tears rolled down her cheeks.

"When are they coming home?" Bob asked.

"I'm not sure," she said. "James said that they would be home soon."

The two agents who had been manning the phones decided to go outside for a smoke. Additional agents were on their way to the house.

"Thank God the kids are okay," said Bob. "I don't know about you, but I could sure use a drink. You go relax on the couch and I'll get the drinks."

As soon as Meg sat down on the couch, Ginger jumped up and cuddled next to her.

Meg wanted to share their good news with their family, but she would have to wait until they were sure that Clair and Tom were safe.

Bob returned with their drinks and sat in the chair next to the couch.

"Those guys are sure taking a long time to have a cigarette," Meg said. "Where are the other agents they were sending?"

Bob walked over and looked out the window. They should have been standing near the front porch, but they were nowhere in sight. He locked the front door and turned to Meg.

"Something isn't right! We need to get out of here now! Do you have a flashlight?"

"I have a flashlight and a .38 revolver in the bedroom. When you're married to an FBI agent, you're always prepared for the worse."

Ginger, who had been sleeping on the couch, started growling. Meg grabbed Ginger and Bob followed her down the hallway to the bedroom. She opened the drawer to the nightstand and retrieved a large flashlight and a Lady Smith and Wesson .38 revolver.

Meg handed the flashlight and the gun to Bob and picked up Ginger. Before they were able to get out of the bedroom, all the lights went out. They heard the shattering of glass. Ginger growled. Meg gently held her snout so she couldn't bark. Bob checked the phone in the bedroom; it was dead.

"Someone's cut the power to the house and phone lines," Bob whispered. "Get behind the bed and stay down!"

Bob locked the bedroom door and used the vanity chair to secure the door. He joined Meg and Ginger behind the bed. He aimed the gun at the bedroom door and handed the flashlight to Meg.

Meg turned the flashlight on and covered it with a pillow.

"If he comes through the door I want to be ready," she explained. "If I can shine the light in his face, it might blind him long enough for you to get a shot at him."

Meg put Ginger under the bed.

"Stay, Ginger," she commanded.

Ginger sensed Meg's unease and stayed under the bed.

The hardwood floor creaked as the intruder walked down the hallway and stopped at the bedroom door. They could see a light under the door. He tried the doorknob. When he realized it was locked, he kicked the door open.

Meg aimed the flashlight at the dark figure coming through the door. Bob shot off two rounds. The intruder turned and ran. Once Bob was in the hallway it was too dark to see the intruder. Meg ran to Bob and handed him the flashlight, but it was too late. The guy had disappeared.

"Damn, I must have missed him!" yelled Bob. "We need some light in here!" Bob found the breaker box and turned on the lights. They ran back to the bedroom.

Meg called for Ginger. Ginger slowly crawled out from under the bed and jumped into Meg's arms.

"Bob, look! There's blood on the floor."

"Well, we aren't bleeding, so I must have hit the SOB," Bob said. "Did you recognize the guy?"

"Everything happened so fast I didn't get a good look at him."

Someone started banging on the front door. Meg looked out the window. It was Agent Cooper, who had gone outside for a smoke. Bob motioned for Meg to move away from the door. Slowly, he opened the door, keeping the gun at his side. Cooper's eyes were glazed over and his shirt was covered with blood. Bob helped him to a chair. He had a nasty cut on the back of his head.

"My partner is still out there!" Cooper said.

"I'll go find him," said Bob.

Meg returned with a wet towel. "Hold the towel on the wound," she ordered. "It will help stop the bleeding."

Bob found Agent Green lying on the ground behind the tree. Blood gushed from a deep wound to his head. Bob checked his pulse. He was unconscious, but alive. Bob ran to the agents' car and used the car radio to call for help. Within minutes, the neighborhood was crawling with Monrovia PD Officers and FBI agents. An ambulance transported the two agents to the ER.

Chapter 20

Sunday, September 17

It had been a long ride home from Big Bear. Clair and Tom, exhausted from their ordeal, had slept all the way home.

"Hey, sleepyheads, wake up. We're almost home," said James.

Clair and Tom sat up. Clair stretched and rubbed her eyes. "I can't wait to see Mom."

However, their excitement would be short-lived.

Police barricades blocked off the street. Hank and James jumped out of the car. A police officer approached them.

"Sorry, sir, but you need to get out of here."

Hank pulled out his ID. "I'm FBI Agent Welch. This is retired Agent Riley and he lives down the street. What the hell is going on?"

"There was a shooting and a couple of FBI agents were injured."

James' heart was in his throat. He ran down the street toward his house. Hank, Clair, and Tom followed close behind.

Crime scene tape surrounded James' house and police officers formed a line to keep curious onlookers at bay.

"Dad, what's going on?" cried Clair.

"You and Tom stay here!" yelled James.

James and Hank entered the house. Meg ran into James' arms.

James kissed Meg. "Thank God you're okay!"

Bob walked over and put his hand on James shoulder. "We're fine," he said. "Not so sure about our visitor! He left a blood trail that goes from the house to the side gate and down the alley. They lost the blood trail by some bushes at the end of the alley. He's lost a lot of blood. He dropped his gun and car keys to a Ford Mustang. Without a ride, he isn't going to get very far."

James and Bob returned to the living room just as Tom and Clair ran through the front door. Meg gave them a big hug.

Clair stood with her hands on her hip, glaring at her father.

James had totally forgotten about Clair and Tom.

James walked over and kissed Clair on the cheek. "You are definitely your mother's daughter. Tom, you have your work cut out for you!"

"I'm just thankful that Clair and Tom are safe," cried Meg. "No more walks around the block!"

Tom put his arms around Clair. "See, babe, exercise is bad!"

Clair pushed him away. "It wasn't the walk that got us in

trouble. It was your stupid idea to go into that creepy old vacant house!"

"Okay, sweetie, you're right."

James laughed. "Tom, you handled that like a pro!"

"Meg," said James, "Bob and I need to talk to Hank. We'll be right back."

"I'm sure we could all use a strong drink and some food," said Meg. "Tom, why don't you make some drinks? A lot of bourbon and a splash of water. Clair and I will work on the food."

****

When James and Bob walked outside, Hank was receiving updates on the injured agents.

"Hank, how are your agents doing?" asked Bob.

"Agent Cooper was treated and sent home. Agent Greene sustained a concussion. They're keeping him in the hospital overnight for observation. He should go home tomorrow."

"That's good news," said Bob. "I have a question. I thought they were sending more agents to protect us? Where in the hell were they?"

"I don't know, but I'm going to find out," said Hank.

****

Meg was still shaken.

"Mom, why don't you sit down and relax," said Clair. "I can finish the sandwiches."

Tom handed Meg a drink.

"What happened tonight?" asked Tom.

Meg downed her drink. "As soon as James and Bob finish talking to Hank, you'll hear the whole story."

****

Bob, James, and Hank joined the group at the kitchen table. Tom made sure they each had a drink. Clair placed a platter of sandwiches in the middle of the table along with a fresh pot of hot coffee. While they ate, Bob and Meg went through the events of the night.

Clair hugged her mother. "No wonder you're so upset. You could've been killed!"

"None of this makes sense," said James.

"What do you mean?" asked Meg.

"The two kidnappers are dead. They were small-time crooks who didn't have a full brain between the two of them. I don't think it was a coincidence that the kids were left alone at a cabin just a few miles from your parents' cabin."

"It wasn't that difficult for Clair and I to escape," said Tom.

"I think they wanted you and Tom to go to the cabin and for us to find you there. It gave them plenty of time to go after Meg and Bob. I'm convinced that we've been stalked for months, starting with the prowler last summer. I am more convinced than ever that the prowler and the guy in the garage are the same person."

"James, do you think that the kidnapping was a diversion to

their real plan?" asked Bob.

"Yes, I do!"

"I hate the thought, but the person behind all this has to be someone who is familiar with your family," Hank said. "Who else would know the comings and goings of the family this weekend and know about your in-laws' cabin?"

The realization that his family was in danger and it could be someone they knew and trusted sent chills up James' spine.

"The local PD is still searching for the guy that was here tonight," Hank said. "Agents will be stationed at your house and Meg's parents' house until we catch the person threatening your family.

"I know that we were trying to keep this quiet, but I think it's time to notify the family. Meg, would you call your parents and let them know what happened and that our agents will be stationed at their house? Make sure they understand that they can't tell anyone.

"Tom, I've notified the FBI in Ohio and they will be assigning agents to your parents' house. I need you to contact your parents and let them know what's going on. Again, they must keep this to themselves."

Meg walked over to Tom. "Come on, Tom, let's go make the calls in the den."

"James, I'm taking off," said Hank. "Everything is under control and I know you can take it from here. I'll call you in the morning."

James shook Hank's hand. "Thanks for all your help."

James watched as Hank drove away.

Chapter 21

Sunday, September 17

The pain was excruciating. The bullet had hit him in the thigh and he was losing a lot of blood. His eyes burned from the sweat that ran down from his brow. He had made his way down the dark alley and was almost to the street when he heard sirens. He was able to crawl behind some bushes before two patrol cars flew down the street. Blood continued to gush from his wound. He had to stop the bleeding. He removed his shirt and tied it above the gunshot wound. He waited for a few minutes before exiting the alley. When he was satisfied that it was safe he crossed the street.

He had parked in a lot next to a bar on Foothill Blvd. It was several blocks from Agent Riley's house. When he finally got to his car, he reached into his pants pocket for his keys. They were gone. He must have dropped them at the house. He had lost a lot of blood and felt weak and was nauseous. There was a large pine tree next to his car. He crawled over to the tree and sat down. All he needed was some rest. He leaned back against the tree and closed his eyes. What he didn't know was the bullet had pierced his femoral artery and he was bleeding out.

****

It was four in the morning when the bar owner finally locked up and walked to his car. He noticed the red 1965 Mustang parked near his car. He didn't see the man by the tree until he walked around to the driver's side of his car. It was obvious that he was dead. He went back to the bar and called the police.

Chapter 22

Sunday, September 17

James was exhausted, but he couldn't sleep. Meg was sound asleep with Ginger snuggled next to her. He carefully rolled out of bed, grabbed his gun and flashlight, and went to the kitchen. He made himself a drink and laid his gun on the table next to him. The thought that a friend of the family could be responsible for this attack on his family was disturbing. Maybe a list of friends, neighbors, and co-workers would help identify possible suspects. He went to the study and sat down at the desk. He was searching through the desk for a scratch pad when Bob walked in the room.

"Couldn't sleep?" asked Bob.

"It's so hard for me to believe that the person attacking my family could be a friend. I decided a list of all our friends might help."

The phone rang, interrupting their conversation.

After a short conversation, James hung up the phone.

"That was Hank," said James. "They found the body of a man in a parking lot next to the Aztec Bar on Foothill Blvd. Looks like he bled out from a gunshot wound. He was next to a red '65 Mustang. One more thing, he has a wound on his leg. Leads me to believe that he was the one stalking me and my family."

Clair and Tom walked into the room.

"Who was that on the phone?" asked Meg.

"That was Hank, they found a man's body in the Aztec Bar parking lot. He's pretty sure it's the guy who tried to attack you and Bob. We also suspect that he was our stalker. Bob and I are going to meet Hank at the scene. Agents are parked out front. We'll be back as soon as we can."

"We'll be fine," said Meg. "Anyway, I have my gun if I need it."

James kissed Meg. "That's my girl."

Clair gave her father a hug.

"We'll be fine," said Tom.

****

James and Bob joined Hank, who was standing by the body.

"Do they know who he is?" asked James

"We found his wallet with his driver's license. The picture on the driver's license matches our dead man. He is Arturo Gallo, twenty-five, from San Francisco.

"We searched the car, but we didn't find the registration. We're going to take the car back to the FBI garage. We can trace the car's owner through the car's VIN number."

James and Bob stayed until the body was removed and the car was towed away. It had been a long and exhausting day. It was time to go home.

Chapter 23

Monday, September 18

The next morning James and Bob went to City Hall to do some research on the old house.

When they returned, Meg was cleaning the kitchen. "What did you find out?" she asked.

"Nothing earth-shattering," said James. "According to county records, the original owners were Gladys and Doris Murphy. When they passed away they left their entire estate to their nephew, Gary Murphy. He's currently living in Oregon. The only thing he's guilty of is failing to respond to written requests from the city to clean up the property. No one, including the kids, knew they were going to go to that house. I'm convinced that the kidnappers were watching and waiting for an opportunity to grab the kids. They just lucked out when the kids went into that house. I'm going to assume we are still being watched. Everyone needs to stay together and report anything that doesn't feel right."

James and Meg started working on a list of all their friends, neighbors, and acquaintances. They even included Clair's friends from high school.

Chapter 24

Tuesday, September 19

Hank called the next morning.

"I ran Arturo's name through the FBI's National Crime Information Center database. He's originally from New York and did time in New York for grand theft auto. He's been in and out of the New York criminal system since the age of twelve."

"We were able to contact his parole officer. He told us that when Arturo was released from parole, he moved to San Francisco to live with his sister, Anna. The parole officer gave us his sister's address and phone number. The coroner was able to notify his sister. She's flying down tomorrow to identify the body. I'm scheduled to meet with her at ten in the morning after she's identified the body."

"Would you mind if I sat in on the interview?" asked James.

"No problem, I'll give you a call," said Hank.

"What do we know about Anna?" asked James.

"Not a whole lot, but what we do know is that she owns a successful clothing boutique in San Francisco. She's clean, never had as much as a traffic ticket. However, we are looking at her business to see where her financing came from and if she has a business partner."

"What about the car?" asked James.

"According to the VIN number, it was reported stolen from a Ford dealer in San Francisco."

"Thanks for the info," said James. "Talk to you later."

Chapter 25

LA County Coroner's Office
Wednesday, September 20

Anna Gallo arrived at the coroner's office the next day. She grabbed the attention of every man in the office. She was tall and slender, with long black hair pulled back in a ponytail. Her olive complexion was flawless. She wore a red jumpsuit covered in bright multicolored butterflies. A pair of black patent leather sling heels completed her outfit.

The coroner escorted her to the viewing area of the morgue. He lifted the sheet from Arturo's face. The color drained from her face and her knees went weak. They escorted her to an interview room and gave her a glass of water.

She looked up when Hank and James entered the room.

"Hello, Miss Gallo, I'm FBI agent Welch and this is Agent Riley. Are you feeling better?"

"Yes, it was just the shock of seeing him like that."

"Do you know what your brother was doing in LA?" asked Hank.

"I didn't know that he had plans to go to LA. When he didn't come home, I called his work. They told me that he hadn't reported to work for two days. I was getting ready to file a missing person's report when the coroner's office called. The coroner told me that he died from a gunshot wound. How did it happen?"

James leaned forward. "He broke into my house and tried to kill my wife and a family friend. Unfortunately for him, my friend was a better shot."

"I can't believe that he would do such a thing. He had been in and out of trouble since he was a teen but he never hurt anyone. His crimes involved auto theft and burglary. Never murder!"

"Do you know if anyone had tried to contact him in the last month or so?"

"He hasn't made any friends since he moved to San Francisco. He'd cut off all ties with the New York crowd and I don't remember him getting any phone calls or letters."

"What about co-workers?"

"Not that I'm aware of. He kept to himself."

"Did he own a gun?"

"If he did, I never saw it. When will they release his body?" she asked. "I want to bury him in our family plot in New York next to our parents."

"You can discuss this with the coroner before you leave," explained Hank. "They will help you make arrangements to move him to New York. Thank you for your cooperation, Miss Gallo. Please let me know if you need anything."

"Thank you. I'm flying back to San Francisco in the morning. Here is my work number. I'm at the boutique most of the time."

After meeting with the coroner to make arrangements to have her brother's remains transferred to New York, she took a taxi back to her hotel.

Chapter 26

Thursday, September 21

The following afternoon Hank received a call from Anna's business partner, Sue Ross.

"Hello Agent Welch, my name is Sue Ross. I'm Anna Gallo's partner and part-owner of the boutique. Anna called me yesterday after she left the coroner's office. She told me she had discovered some information that could get her killed. She also told me she needed to disappear for a while, but would call me this morning and let me know she was safe, but I haven't heard from her. She said to call you if anything happened to her. I am really worried."

"Miss Ross, I appreciate the phone call. I am going to try to catch a flight to San Francisco tonight or early tomorrow morning. Until I get there, you need to be careful and call the police if you feel threatened in any way."

Chapter 27

Thursday, September 21

James put down the telephone. "That was Hank. There's a new development on the case that he wants to share with us. He's on his way."

When he arrived, they gathered around the kitchen table. Hank told them about the phone call from Sue Ross, the possibility that Anna was in trouble, and his plans for a quick trip to San Francisco.

"I want to go with you," said James.

"James, your family is still in danger," said Hank.

"Have you forgotten that you are the one who placed agents outside our house to protect us?"

"I haven't forgotten, and I also remember that Arturo Gallo managed to get by my agents and attacked Meg and Bob. You need to stay here and protect them. Another issue is that you are retired. There is no way that the agency would allow you to go. It's too much of a liability. I promise that I will keep you informed."

"Okay," said James. "I know you're right, but I don't have to like it."

Chapter 28

Friday, September 22

Hank arrived at seven in the morning. His first stop was the boutique, but it was closed. He called Sue's personal number, but there wasn't an answer.

He decided to check Anna's apartment. When he arrived, he found the door ajar. He pulled his gun and carefully pushed the door open. The place was a mess. He decided to start his search in Anna's room. He had just started checking her closet when he heard a noise in the living room. Gun drawn, he quietly made his way down the hallway. He stopped at the end of the hallway and peeked into the living room. A man was going through Anna's desk.

"FBI!" yelled Hank. "Put your hands where I can see them and turn around!"

James turned around.

"What the hell are you doing here?" asked Hank. "I could have shot you."

"I'm sorry, but I couldn't stay away."

Hank didn't want to admit that he was glad to see James. "Well, since you're here you might as well help me go through this mess," he said.

"Don't worry. Remember I came on my own," said James.

They searched through Anna and Arturo's bedrooms. Anna's closet was full of clothes, shoes, and purses, but Arturo's closet was empty. It appeared that she planned on returning.

Their next stop was the warehouse where Arturo had worked.

At the warehouse, they talked to the manager. He told them Arturo had worked there for close to a year. About two weeks ago, Arturo had asked for time off to take care some personal business. That was the last time he had heard from him.

Chapter 29

Friday, September 22

Meg, Bob, Clair, and Tom had finished going through the case files Hank had left with them. Unfortunately, they had come up empty-handed.

"I think James was on to something when he suspected that the murder case in Alaska was behind this assault on your family," said Bob.

"That was twenty-eight years ago," said Meg.

"Mom, I never heard the details of that case. I know that Uncle Bob was the commissioner in Alaska. Why was Uncle George with them?"

Bob spoke up. "Two of the murder victims were your Uncle George's brother and sister-in-law. In 1939, Alaska was a territory of the US and the FBI had jurisdiction over all criminal investigations in Alaska. Your dad was assigned to investigate the murders of four people. He actually had us all convinced that he was a dirty cop working with the bad guys. They were surprised when your dad turned on them. The two murder suspects died in a shoot-out with your dad, myself, George, and George's brother, Ron."

"Why would they wait this long?" asked Meg.

"I think we can speculate that we are dealing with an unstable person," said Bob. "A family member who blames James for everything that has gone bad in his or her life."

"Hank was going to have a couple of his agents check out any surviving relatives," said Bob. "We'll check with Hank when he gets back."

Meg was relieved when James called; however, she was still angry with James for following Hank to San Francisco.

"We're at the San Francisco Airport," said James. "We're scheduled to land at nine at LAX. I'll fill you in on the trip when I get home."

Chapter 30

Friday, September 22

It was ten when James and Hank walked through the door, tired and hungry.

They all gathered around the kitchen table, eating and listening to James and Hank tell about their adventures in San Francisco.

"Hank, did you ever get information on the surviving family members of the suspects from the Alaska murders?" asked James.

"I just got the report before leaving for San Francisco," he said. "The report is at my office. I can bring it over tomorrow. I still have my doubts about that case having anything to do with all of this, but it can't hurt to take a look."

"We have gone through all the case files," explained Bob. "We haven't found anything."

James spoke up. "We have checked out all our friends and neighbors and have come up empty."

"The Alaska case was unique," James continued. "What was surprising was the fact that the murder rate in the Dutch Hills was really low. When four people were murdered in one day it was a big deal. The majority of the prospectors were ready and willing to help us catch the killers. They weren't sad when the suspects died in that shoot-out."

"Okay," said Hank. "Then where do Arturo and Anna fit into the picture?"

"That's a really a good question," said James.

Chapter 31

Saturday, September 23

Hank dropped off the file the next day. "I haven't looked at it," he said. "I'll leave that job to you. Let me know if you find anything in the file."

"We'll keep you posted," said James.

James and Bob went into the den and started going through the file.

"There were four people involved in this mess," said James. "Perry Jackson, Ken Cooper, Richard Hill, and Swede Erikson.

"I think we can rule out Perry and Ken. I didn't have anything to do with their deaths; Richard Hill killed them. I think we can rule out Richard Hill. According to the file, they couldn't find any relatives to claim his body.

"The only one left is Swede Erikson. He left behind a wife and son. Swede's given name was Vilhelm Erikson. It says in the file that he and his wife, Alice, were separated, but never divorced. She claimed his body and he was buried in a cemetery in Seattle."

"Remember, I live and work in Seattle," said Bob. "I have staff that does all the research for my books. If you don't mind, I can make a few calls and see what they can come up with."

"Sounds good to me," said James.

Bob headed to the study and James joined Meg and the kids in the kitchen to make lunch. Bob returned to the kitchen a few minutes later.

"We're all set. Now all we have to do is wait and hope they find some information on this family."

Chapter 32

Tuesday, September 26

A few days later, Bob received a call from his contact.

"Okay, this is what they found. When Alice left Swede, she and their son, Sven, moved to Seattle to live with her sister, May Brady. May sold her house and moved to San Francisco several years ago. But one of the neighbors in Seattle, Mrs. Anderson, was a close friend of May's. She told my contact that Alice gave birth to a baby girl a few months after she moved in with May. She named her Kristina."

"Maybe that's the reason she never filed for divorce," said Meg.

"You might be right. May told Mrs. Anderson that Swede and Alice were trying to reconcile. She said Swede had told Alice that he was waiting for a big payday and would be home as soon as he got everything squared away. Unfortunately, his big payday went south. He made a big mistake when he got mixed up with Richard Hill. It got him killed."

"How sad," said Meg "He died trying to get his family back."

Bob continued. "May was a widow and never had children. She was delighted to have Alice and the children living with her. May was a secretary at a law office and helped Alice get a file clerk job. Alice tried to move forward, but she never recovered from Swede's death. In 1946, she committed suicide. Hung herself in the garage."

"How old were the children when Alice died?" asked Meg.

"Sven was eleven and Kristina was six," said Bob. "Sven found his mother."

"How awful," said Meg. "How does a child recover from that kind of trauma?"

"Mrs. Anderson said she thought it odd that they didn't have a service for Alice. I asked if she had been buried next to Swede. She said she didn't believe they had buried Alice because she was cremated. A few months after Alice died, May sold the house, quit her job, and moved to San Francisco with the children."

"Did May adopt the children?" asked Meg.

"According to Mrs. Anderson, May wanted to adopt the children, but the children didn't want to be adopted. They wanted to keep their family name. She said May did everything for those children, but in the end, they broke her heart. When Sven turned eighteen, he joined the military. After his discharge, he moved to New York, got involved in an auto theft ring, and ended up in prison. Sound familiar?"

"Sure does," said James. "I would bet that Sven and Arturo were both involved in the same auto theft ring and served time together at Rikers. That would connect Sven to Arturo and his sister. I'll see if Hank can run Sven's name through the database and confirm if he did any time at Rikers."

"What happened to Kristina?" asked Meg.

"Kristina graduated from college with a degree in accounting. The day she graduated, she packed her bag and walked out. May never heard from her again.

"Mrs. Anderson and May kept in contact after May moved to San Francisco. They wrote to each other every month and occasionally talked on the phone. May's letters were always upbeat and she never indicated she was having problems. Then, about five months ago, Mrs. Anderson stopped receiving letters from May. She tried calling May, but her phone had been disconnected. Alarmed, Mrs. Anderson contacted the SFPD and requested a welfare check. The police reported that May wasn't at the house. The house was clean and neat and all of her clothes and other personal items were in the house. There wasn't any evidence of a break-in or struggle. It was like she had vanished into thin air. They still haven't found her. It's still an open investigation."

"That is just bizarre," said James.

"It gets even more bizarre," said Bob.

"Just as my contact was leaving Mrs. Anderson's house, the mailman delivered a manila envelope. It was postmarked from San Francisco and didn't have a return address. When she opened the envelope, she found a letter inside. It was the last letter she had sent to May and it had been opened."

"Do you think May sent the letter back to Mrs. Anderson?" asked James.

"It's possible that May was letting her friend know that she was still alive. On the other hand, Mrs. Anderson had her return address on the envelope, so anyone could have sent it. But that doesn't make much sense."

"Do the police know about the letter?" asked James.

"Not yet," said Bob. "Mrs. Anderson has graciously agreed to loan us all of May's letters, including the one that was returned to her. My contact is sending them special delivery and we should get them tomorrow."

"I'm concerned that Mrs. Anderson might be in danger," said James.

"I had the same concerns," said Bob. "She is going to stay with her daughter in Oregon until this is resolved. I just don't understand why Sven and Kristina severed all ties with May. She raised them like her own children and they abandoned her. I just hope the letters will provide us with some clues to help find her."

Chapter 33

Wednesday, September 27

A package containing thirty letters arrived the next morning. James and Bob recruited Meg, Clair, and Tom to help go through the letters. After several hours, tired and frustrated, they stopped for a break. They sat around the table eating and discussing the letters.

"The San Francisco/New York connection is the key to finding answers to May and Anna's disappearance," said James. "We know that Sven and Arturo were involved in a car theft ring in New York and went to prison. Arturo is dead and we don't know where Sven is or if he is alive. San Francisco was the last place of residence for Anna and May before they disappeared. There has to be a connection."

"Bob, I think we need to go to San Francisco and do our own search of May's house," said James.

"When do we leave?" asked Bob.

"Meg, could you and the kids continue to go through the letters?" asked James. "We won't be there that long. All we're going to do is take another look at May's house."

"Are you going to fly?" she asked.

"I think it would be better if we drove," he said. "It's a long drive, but I like the freedom of having my own car."

Chapter 34

Thursday, September 28

James and Bob left at four thirty the next morning, arriving in San Francisco around noon.

They stopped for a quick lunch and then drove to May's house.

According to Bob's contacts, the police had finished searching the house and had secured the property. May's neighbor had a key to the house.

They pulled up to the house. While Bob went next door to get the key, James climbed the stairs to the front porch. He tried the doorknob and to his surprise the door opened. He turned and saw Bob coming up the sidewalk. Bob joined him on the porch.

"Quiet," said James. "The door isn't locked."

James pulled his gun from his shoulder holster and opened the door. They moved slowly through each room of the house.

"Did you hear that?" asked James.

"Sounds like it's coming from the basement," said Bob.

The basement door was ajar and they could see a light.

They moved slowly down the steps to the basement. A dark figure was rummaging through a box.

"Don't move!" yelled James. "I have a gun. I need you to put your hands up and turn around real slow."

"Nice to see you again, Mr. Riley."

"Anna, what are you doing here?" asked James.

"I think the same thing that you're doing here," she said. "Looking for May."

"How do you know May?" asked James.

"We met at Rikers. I went to visit Arturo and she was visiting Sven."

"We bonded and corresponded for several months. When I made the decision to move to San Francisco she invited me to stay with her until I found my own place. She was such a wonderful woman."

"It was our understanding that she didn't have any contact with Sven after he joined the army," said Bob.

"She didn't want anyone to know that Sven was in prison," she said. "I think she always blamed herself that Sven and Kristina were so troubled. May was on a limited income so she was only able to visit him once. I just lucked out I was there that day when I met her. I was the only one who knew about Sven."

"Your friend at the boutique said you had gone into hiding because you were in danger."

"When I returned from LA, I started to go through my brother's things. I found a disturbing letter from Sven. In the letter, he warned Arturo that if he didn't get the 'job' done, he would kill me. The next day I called May and asked her if she had heard from Sven. She said she had not seen him since her visit to the prison. I've been hiding out with a friend in Santa Cruz.

"I called May to make sure that she was okay, but she never answered. I decided to come to the house and check on her, but she wasn't here. I've been looking for anything that might lead me to her. I found a box labeled 'Alice' and one for 'May.' They contained letters, pictures, and documents. I'm so worried that Sven did something awful to May."

"Did May ever say anything about Kristina?" asked James.

"Only that she hadn't seen or heard from her since the day she packed up and left."

"If we leave now we should be home by ten tonight," said James. "Anna, I want you to come home with us, where we can keep you safe. We'll take the boxes with us."

Chapter 35

Friday, September 29
Riley House

The next morning, everyone gathered in the living room and started going through the boxes from May's house.

They found letters to Alice and Sven from Swede. None of the letters indicated that Alice had known about the mess Swede had gotten himself into. They found several photos of Alice, Swede, and Sven when they lived in Alaska. They found Alice and Swede's marriage certificate and Swede's death certificate. What they didn't find were birth certificates for Alice, Sven, and Kristina.

Anna was going through the photos and found Sven's military picture. "He's really young in this picture, but he hasn't changed that much," she said.

James studied the photo. There was something familiar about him, probably because he resembled Swede.

"You aren't going to believe this!" yelled Anna.

She handed a photo of two infant girls to James. On the back was written, "Alice and May, born June 1, 1917."

"They were twins!" she yelled. "May and Alice were twins!"

They continued to go through the photos. They found pictures of Alice and May when they were teenagers. The only difference was that Alice was slightly taller than May.

Bob made a call to Mrs. Anderson, who confirmed that Alice and May were twins. She told Bob that Alice had a brown birthmark on the inside of her wrist.

"She could have shared this information," said James.

"I guess she thought that it wasn't important," said Bob.

"Wait a minute," said James. "Remember how Mrs. Anderson couldn't understand why the children were so mean to May after everything that she did for them? May's house was paid for, so why sell and move to San Francisco? What if Alice murdered May and took May's identity."

"Wouldn't they have identified her through her fingerprints?" asked Meg.

"Not if the family confirmed her identity. The neighbor told us that Alice was cremated."

"Why would anyone kill their sister?" asked Meg.

"Alice needed money and could easily pass for her sister," said James. "She also needed to get out of Seattle. She would have been able to clean out May's bank accounts and sell her house without anyone suspecting a thing. She and the children moved to San Francisco. No need to adopt your own children."

"James, do you think that the children knew what their

mother did?" asked Anna.

"I find it hard to believe that the children didn't know what their mother had done. If anyone could tell May and Alice apart, it would have been the children."

"So, it must have been Alice that I met at Rikers," said Anna.

Chapter 36

Saturday, September 30

James was convinced that Sven, Alice, and Kristine were working together to destroy his family. He had to find them.

It was time to tell Hank about their trip to San Francisco. Hopefully, Hank would be able to get some info on Sven and Kristine from the database.

James still hadn't heard from Hank and decided to call the house. He attempted to call several times but no one answered.

"Maybe they're out for the evening," said Meg. "I've been told that some couples actually go out on Saturday nights!"

"You sure know how to make a guy feel guilty. I think I'll go over to the house. If they aren't there, I'll leave a note for him to call me."

"I'll go with you," said Bob.

"Meg, make sure you lock all the doors and windows," said James. "I'll alert the officers outside."

"We know the routine," said Meg. "Remember, I have my gun and I know how to use it."

Chapter 37

Saturday, September 30

Hank's car was in the driveway when they pulled up to the house. The house was dark and the porch light was off. They always kept the porch light on at night. James went to the garage and shone the flashlight through the window. Tina's car was gone.

"They probably took Tina's car," said Bob.

"You're probably right. I'll just leave a note on the front door."

As they approached the front door, they noticed it was slightly open.

"Forgetting to leave the lights on happens," said James. "Hank would never leave the front door open!"

James pulled his revolver from his shoulder holster and handed the flashlight to Bob. He pushed the door open and used his jacket to turn the doorknob. He stepped into the living room. He tried the light switch, but the power appeared to be off. Bob found the breaker box and turned the lights on. They saw a light under the den door and heard a beeping sound.

In the den they found Hank on the floor behind the desk with the phone receiver next to him. Blood gushed from a wound on the back of his head. James checked his pulse.

"Thank God, he's still alive!" yelled James.

James pulled out his handkerchief and carefully picked up the receiver and called the police. Had Hank interrupted a burglary? Where was Tina?

Chapter 38

Saturday, September 30

The Pasadena PD and paramedics were the first to respond, followed by FBI Special Agent John Richards.

James watched as the ambulance left the scene, lights flashing and sirens blaring.

Richards walked over to James and Bob. "Looks like someone is trying to ruin your retirement plans," he told James.

James shook his hand. "It sure looks that way," he said.

"They're taking Hank to Arcadia Methodist," said Richards. "He has blunt force trauma to the back of the head. Have you seen his wife and son?"

"No, Tina wasn't home when we got here. Hank told me that Daniel went back to college last week. He goes to college in Santa Barbara."

"Why did you come over here tonight?"

"As you're aware, Hank has been in charge of the investigation into my daughter's kidnapping and the assault on my wife. Bob and I took a trip to San Francisco and discovered some interesting information. I was hoping Hank could use the database to get some info on a couple of people. I called several times, but he didn't answer. I decided to come over and leave a note. When we got here the lights were off and the front door was open. Someone had turned off the main switch. We turned on the lights and found Hank in the den."

"What people?" asked Richards.

"Do you remember the murder case that I worked on in Alaska?"

"Yes, but wasn't that in 1939!"

James explained he was convinced the motive for the attack on his family was revenge. He explained what they had found so far, giving their theory about Alice and May.

"So, you think that May is really Alice and that she and her children are after your family?" asked Richards.

"I know it sounds crazy," said James. "The guy who tried to kill Bob and Meg was Arturo Gallo. He and Sven Erickson were involved in the same car theft ring in New York and served time together in Rikers. I was going to see if Hank could find information on Sven in the database and get a copy of Sven's booking photo."

"It doesn't appear to be a burglary," said Richards. "You said that the phone rang when you called. What time was that?"

"It was around five thirty."

"I'm guessing that when he opened the door, he heard the

phone ringing. He rushed to the den to answer the phone and left the front door open. He picked up the phone too late and missed the call. He probably still had the phone in his hand when he was hit from behind. He must have knocked some papers onto the floor when he fell. What time did you and Bob get here?"

"I didn't look at my watch, but I would guess around six forty-five. It's possible that the attacker was still here when we got here and went out the back door."

"We checked the back door and it was unlocked. We're checking for fingerprints on the back door. At least we have a timeline. If we're right that this wasn't a burglary, we have to be concerned about Hank's safety. When the assailant finds out that Hank is still alive, he could come back to finish the job. We've teamed up with the Arcadia PD and have men stationed throughout the hospital. We're going to do whatever it takes to protect Hank."

"I know that I'm officially retired, but Hank is my friend. I would like to help with this case and I can legally carry a firearm. I'm convinced that Hank was attacked because he was helping me."

"I don't have a problem with you working with us. You have your PI license and you're representing the family. Right?"

"Absolutely!"

"Anyway, I can learn from your expertise and I owe you one for recommending me for your job."

Just then a car pulled up to the house. It was Tina.

James walked over to Tina's car.

"What's going on?" she asked.

"Tina, I need you to stay calm. Someone tried to kill Hank, but they weren't successful. He sustained a severe head injury. They took him to Arcadia Methodist Hospital."

"Why would someone hurt Hank!" she cried.

Richards walked over to Tina as she got out of the car. "Tina, I'm so sorry about Hank. I do need to ask you a question before you go to the hospital. When was the last time you saw Hank?"

"This morning at breakfast. He decided to go to the office this morning. It's quiet on Saturdays and he can get caught up on his paperwork. He called me around two and told me that he would be working until five. I decided to go grocery shopping and get some wine and steaks for dinner. I should have been here for him!"

"I'm glad you weren't home," said Richards. "We could have had two victims."

"Do you think that Daniel and I are in danger?"

"Right now, I believe Hank was the only target. However, if you or Daniel had gotten in the way you could've been collateral damage. Until we're sure, we need to keep you and Daniel safe. I need the contact information for the college."

Tina wrote down the information.

"I don't want to tell Daniel about his dad until I talk to his doctor. I'll call Daniel from the hospital."

"We can go ahead and set up security at the college without telling Daniel. Just let me know when you tell him and if he wants to come home. We will make sure he gets home safely."

James walked over to Tina. "Tina, Bob and I are ready to take you to the hospital."

****

James and Bob had been gone for a couple of hours and Meg was getting anxious. James finally called. She was relieved to hear his voice.

James told her what had happened and that Tina would be staying with them at the hospital. "They just took him into surgery. We're going to stay with Tina. It's going to be a long night."

"Just keep me informed and be careful," said Meg. "Please give Tina my love."

Chapter 39

Sunday, October 1

James and Bob returned home the next morning.

"Where is Tina?" asked Meg.

"She insisted on staying with Hank. There are police and FBI agents all over that hospital, including the parking lot, so she's in good hands. We decided to come home and get some rest. We're going back this afternoon."

"How's Hank doing?" she asked.

"He's in critical but stable condition. It will be touch-and-go for a few days."

"Is Daniel coming home?"

"No," said James. "I only heard one side of the conversation, but I think that Daniel hung up on her. Tina was visibly shaken."

"Can I go to the hospital with you this afternoon?" asked Meg. "I know that Tina and I aren't that close, but she might feel more comfortable talking to another woman."

"I think that's a good idea."

"I'll stay here with Clair and Tom," said Bob.

Chapter 40

Sunday, October 1

James and Meg arrived at the ICU at one that afternoon. Tina was sitting by Hank's bed holding his hand.

Meg gave Tina a hug.

"Meg, how kind of you to come," said Tina.

"How's he doing?" asked James.

"His vital signs are good and he's been moving his legs."

"Tina, have you had anything to eat?" asked James.

"No, I haven't," she said.

"Meg, why don't you girls go to the cafeteria and get something to eat? I'll sit with Hank."

"What if he wakes up while I'm gone?" asked Tina.

"I'll send someone to get you. I promise."

Tina reluctantly agreed.

****

Meg and Tina evaluated the food choices and decided to go with a salad and coffee. They found a table at the back of the room so they could have some privacy. Although Hank and James were close friends, Meg and Tina had never developed a friendship. The last time they had seen each other was last year at the annual Christmas party.

Tears ran down Tina's face. "I can't believe someone would want to hurt Hank! He's such a good man. Meg, I have to use the restroom."

"Do you want me to go with you?" asked Meg.

"No, I'll be fine."

Meg decided this wasn't a good time to ask Tina about Daniel.

****

Meg checked her watch. It had been fifteen minutes and Tina hadn't returned. Just as Meg was getting ready to check on Tina, James walked into the cafeteria.

"Is Hank alright?" she asked.

"He's still the same," said James. "Since you and Tina were down here I thought I would join you. I really need some coffee. Where's Tina?"

"She went to the restroom about fifteen minutes ago. I was worried and was just getting ready to check on her."

James waited in the hallway while Meg checked the restroom.

Meg opened the door. "Tina isn't in there," she said. "There's something you need to see."

She led him to one of the stalls, where she had found an empty syringe.

"We need to keep everyone out of here," said James. "Meg, go to the cafeteria and use the in-house phone to call the ICU. Tell them what happened and that Hank may be in danger."

James was surprised when he saw Richards exit the elevator.

Richards walked over to James. "I was in the ICU when Meg called."

"No one's been in or out of the restroom. You might run into some angry women that I had to turn away."

"Thanks for securing the crime scene. Forensics should be here any minute. We're going on the assumption that Tina's been abducted. The Arcadia PD officers are helping our agents search the hospital and parking garage."

A police officer ran in holding a purse. "We found this purse in an empty parking space. Mrs. Welch's wallet and driver's license were in the purse."

"I guess it's no longer an assumption."

Chapter 41

Sunday, October 1

James and Meg arrived home to a barrage of questions. James went through the events of the evening.

"Who would want to hurt Hank or Tina?" asked Bob.

"Hank is leading the investigation into the attack on my family. Maybe he found some information on the person responsible for the attacks and whoever is behind all this needed to shut him up. That doesn't explain why Tina was abducted. She goes out to get steak and wine for a romantic dinner and comes home to find out her husband has been attacked. Now she's been abducted and God only knows what has happened to her! I feel like this is all my fault."

"You know that Hank would have taken on this investigation even if you hadn't asked for his help," said Bob.

Meg spoke up. "Didn't you tell me that Hank only drinks bourbon and water and that Tina doesn't drink alcohol? Why would she buy wine?"

"You're right," said James. "Maybe she wasn't being completely honest with us. I think we need to take another trip to Hank's house."

"James," Meg said with a grimace, "I don't think that's a good idea. It's too dangerous."

"We'll be fine. I'll call Richards and have him meet us there. I have a gun and there's a patrolman watching Hank's house. We won't go into the house until Richards gets there."

"James, promise me that you'll call me."

"I promise."

****

James and Bob were startled when they pulled up to the house. The patrol car was gone and the house was dark.

"Where's the patrol car? I'm sure that Richards asked the Pasadena PD for a patrol car to be assigned to Hank's house until further notice."

"That's what I remember," said Bob. "Didn't they leave a light on in the living room?"

"Yes, they did and they left the front and back porch lights on."

"I feel like I'm in a B mystery movie," Bob whispered.

Richards pulled up a few minutes later and James walked to his car.

"I thought there was going to be a patrol car assigned to watch the house?" asked James.

"There was," said Richards.

"Lights were all out when we got here."

The three men approached the front door. The front door was unlocked and the lightbulb was missing from the porch light.

"I've got a couple of flashlights in the car," said Richards.

When Richards returned he told them that he had requested a backup.

They decided to search the perimeter of the house for any signs of a break-in. They moved quietly down the side of the house and into the backyard. Many of the old homes in the San Gabriel Valley had basements and Hank's house was no exception. They were surprised that the light was on in the basement. James and Bob waited on the side of the house while Richards crawled over to the window.

Richards returned a few minutes later. "I can hear voices, but the window is too dirty to see anything. It sounded like a man and woman talking."

Shouldn't your backup be here by now?" asked James.

"Yes," said Richards. "I'm going to go back to the car and radio the dispatcher. Don't do anything until I get back."

It had been several minutes and Richards hadn't returned. James and Bob decided to check on him. When they got to Richards' car, Richards' was laying on the ground next to the open car door, holding the back of his head. The car radio had been ripped from the dashboard.

James ran over to him. "Are you okay? What the hell

happened?"

"The last thing I remember was unlocking the car door."

"Apparently, someone doesn't want more cops here," said James.

"I'm fine," said Richards. "Where's my gun?"

They searched the area around the car and under the car. Bob finally found it wedged behind the left front tire. He handed it to Richards.

"Thanks, Bob," said Richards.

Richards took the lead. They entered the front door and moved slowly through the house until they saw the light under the basement door. Richards reached up and turned the doorknob. The door was unlocked and it was eerily silent. When they reached the basement floor they saw the body of a woman lying facedown on the floor next to a rollaway bed in the corner of the basement. Blood oozed from what appeared to be blunt force trauma to the back of her head. Blood spatter was on the walls and floor. She didn't have a pulse and her body was cold. They searched the basement for a weapon, but came up empty. The murderer must have taken it with him.

"I would guess that she is in her late forties or early fifties," said James.

"Look, Bob," said James. "She has a birthmark on her right wrist. I think we've found Alice. What was she doing in Hank's basement?"

"I'm going to go upstairs and find a phone," said Richards. "I'll be back in a minute."

Richards returned a bit bewildered. "Apparently, someone identifying himself as an FBI agent called the Pasadena PD and told them that we no longer required a patrol car at this location."

"I still can't figure out how Hank and Tina fit into the picture," Bob said.

"I don't know," said James. "I'm as confused as you are. I guess we need to go back and review all of our evidence. I'll let you know if we find anything."

Chapter 42

Monday, October 2

They gathered in the living room and meticulously went through all of their data. They couldn't find anything that linked Hank and Tina to Swede's family.

"I just thought of something," said Meg. "Swede's daughter's name was Kristina. She could be using a nickname. Tina is a common nickname for Kristina."

"I had totally forgotten," said Anna. "When May, I mean Alice, and I were visiting Arturo and Sven at Rikers, Sven asked how Tina was doing. I thought he was asking about a girlfriend, but it must have been Kristina that he was referring to."

"Could Tina Welch actually be Kristina Erickson?"

"It's a possibility," said James. "Maybe Hank found out and Tina was behind the attack on Hank. Was Tina really abducted or was this a smokescreen to make her look like another victim?"

"I'm convinced that Alice had been planning revenge on me, and anyone close to me, since the day Swede was killed," said James. "She killed her own sister to get the money she needed to finance her plan. She needed her children to help her carry out her plan and it appears that they've been loyal to her."

"At least, until now," said Bob. "I think that Sven and Kristina killed Alice. If Tina is really Kristina, why would she want to give up the life that she has? Maybe she wanted out and Alice came here to confront her. It's possible that she killed Alice to protect her family."

"Sven and Kristina were the only ones who knew that Alice murdered May," said Meg. That's an awful secret to keep all these years. It had to have had a psychological effect on them."

"Unfortunately, Sven and Kristina, aka Tina, have the answers and they're both missing," said Tom.

"Their plan seemed to be going well," said James. "They hired Red and Virgil to kidnap Clair and Tom to get me out of town. While Hank and I were in Big Bear searching for the kids, Arturo was supposed to kill Meg. That's when their plan started going south."

"Maybe that's when Tina started to get nervous," said Tom.

Clair hugged Meg. "I am so lucky to have you and Dad."

"I'm beginning to think that Sven is the dangerous one and his next victim could be Daniel."

Richards called a few minutes later to tell James that Hank was awake and alert.

"I told him what had happened at the hospital and that we suspected Tina had been abducted. I also told him that we were keeping Daniel safe."

"How did Hank take the news?" asked James.

"Not well," said Richards. "He was so upset they had to give him a shot to calm him down. Before he fell asleep, he asked to see you."

"Thanks, Richards, I'll go to the hospital first thing in the morning."

Chapter 43

Tuesday, October 3

The next morning, James found Hank sitting up in bed, picking at his breakfast.

He pulled a chair next to Hank's bed. "How are you doing?" he asked Hank.

"I feel like I'm living in a nightmare. My wife is missing and I'm worried about Daniel. He's our only child. Tina has been overprotective with him since the day he was born. She does everything for him. She's been upset with me since I insisted that Daniel should go away to college. He's going to fall apart if anything happens to Tina."

"Do you remember anything from the day you were attacked?" asked Hank.

"Things are starting to come back to me. I remember opening the front door, the phone was ringing. I rushed to the den and picked up the phone, but the caller had already hung up. That's the last thing I remember."

"That explains why the phone was on the floor next to you.

Hank, we don't think this was a burglary."

"Do you think someone tried to kill me?"

"It's possible. The front door was open when Bob and I got there. We think the attacker was waiting outside and must have followed you into the house."

"I don't remember anything after I answered the phone. I had my gun on me when I got home. Did they find it?"

"Maybe one of the agents picked it up. I'll check with Richards. Hank, I need to ask some questions about Tina. I promise I'll explain later."

"Will it help find Tina?"

"Maybe."

"Okay."

"How did you meet Tina?"

"We met when I worked at the San Francisco office. She worked in the accounting office where I got my taxes done. She was much younger than me, so I was surprised when she went out with me. We only dated for a few months when she agreed to marry me. Daniel was born eleven months later. In fact, Tina was the one who pushed me to transfer to the LA office."

"What about Tina's family?"

"She was an only child. Her parents were killed in a car accident in Seattle shortly after she graduated from college. She moved to San Francisco and went to work at the accounting office where I met her. All she ever wanted was her own family.

Daniel and I are her whole world. I'm so worried about her. I can't imagine why anyone would want to hurt her."

"They're using all their resources to find her," said James. "What was Tina's maiden name?"

"Brady."

"Did Tina ever mention a woman named May or Alice?"

"No," said Hank.

"What about a man named Sven?"

"Never heard of him. Who are these people?"

"Hank, I will explain all this to you when I have more information. Promise me that you will let me know if you remember anything."

"You'll be the first to know."

"Do you mind if I take another look at your house?"

"Not at all. There's a key hidden in the eve above the front door. I don't know what you're hoping to find, but good luck."

What James didn't want to find was another dead body.

****

It was noon when James and Bob arrived at Hank's house. They parked down the street and walked to the house. They did a quick walk around the house, making sure that all doors and windows remained secured.

James found the key and they entered the living room. He locked the door once they were inside.

"Just in case Tina comes back to the house," said James.

James had never been to Hank's house during the day. He was taken aback by the bright, sunny living room. It felt like a façade, hiding the evil and deception of a house that had been the scene of a vicious attack and murder.

They were hoping to find the missing birth certificates or, even better, a diary or journal. Tina might have kept some family documents that Hank was unaware of. They started in the study. The room was filled with rich dark wood bookshelves, a large rolltop desk, and burgundy leather furniture. A large Persian area rug covered the hardwood floors.

"I didn't realize that FBI supervisors made enough money to live like this," said Bob.

"They don't," said James. "Hank inherited a substantial estate from his parents. They used some of the money to buy this house."

They started in the study and then moved through each room in the house, but didn't find anything.

The basement was the next target. James flicked on the light switch at the top of the basement stairs and they slowly made their way down the stairs. The basement was damp and musty. It was filled with all the unwanted stuff that people couldn't bring themselves to throw away.

They had just started going through boxes when Bob yelled and jumped back.

"Black widow coming down the wall!" he yelled.

James started laughing. "You can relax, it's a daddy longlegs. It can't hurt you."

"I hate spiders!"

James motioned for Bob to be quiet. They heard the hardwood floors creaking above them.

"Someone's upstairs," whispered James. "I hope they don't decide to come down here!"

They took cover under the stairs. James pulled out his gun and they waited. The only weapon Bob could find was a shovel. It would have to do.

They heard voices and then they heard two shots and the front door slam.

They rushed up the stairs and opened the door. Tina lay on the floor in the kitchen. She had been shot, but she was alive. One of the bullets had hit her in the chest. The second shot grazed the side of her head. She was losing a lot of blood from the chest wound. Bob called for an ambulance and then called Richards.

James grabbed a towel from the bathroom and used it to put pressure on the wound. "You're are going to be fine," he told her.

She grabbed his hand.

"Tina, who shot you?"

But Tina was too weak. She lost consciousness before she could identify her shooter.

Chapter 44

Tuesday, October 3

It was late afternoon when the crime scene was finally cleared. Tina had been transported to the same hospital where Hank was recovering.

Richards and James agreed that James should be the one to tell Hank about Tina.

James and Bob decided it wasn't necessary for both of them to go to the hospital. Richards volunteered to give Bob a ride to James' house. James was getting ready to leave for the hospital when they heard a voice.

"What's going on here?"

They were shocked to see Daniel standing in the doorway.

"Where's the officer who was protecting you?" asked James.

"Still at the college, I was able to sneak out and drive home. I've been worried about my mom. Since no one was telling me anything, I decided to come down and see for myself."

"Daniel, you were so upset about your dad that we didn't want to make it worse. I'm sorry, that was a mistake. You aren't a child and we should have kept you in the loop. Your mom has suffered two gunshot wounds by an unknown assailant. She's on her way to the hospital. She's alive, but she's lost a lot of blood. I was just getting ready to go to the hospital to give your dad the news about your mom. You can go with me and I'll fill you in on everything that's going on. Your dad really needs you."

At the hospital, James and Daniel were told that Hank had been moved to a regular room. Their first stop was the ER to check on Tina. When they requested to see Tina, they were asked to wait.

A few minutes later, an ER doctor came out to talk to them. "She's lost a lot of blood and hasn't regained consciousness. The bullet to her chest barely missed her heart. We are concerned that she is bleeding internally. We are prepping her for surgery."

James told the doctor they would be in Hank's room and asked that they keep them updated on her condition. He called Richards and was assured there would be a police officer providing Tina security until further notice.

"Daniel, your dad knows that your mom was kidnapped, but he doesn't know about the shooting. We need to tell him."

Hank was sitting up in bed. His face lit up when he saw his son. "Daniel, what are you doing here?"

Daniel gave his father a hug. "When I couldn't get ahold of Mom, I decided to come home."

"The important thing is that you are here now," said Hank.

"James, did you find anything at the house?"

"We didn't find anything, but something happened while we were there," said James.

James told Hank about the attack on Tina and that the shooter had gotten away before being identified.

"She's in the ER, they're getting her ready for surgery. They're going to call us here with any updates on her condition. Hank, she's in bad shape."

The color drained from Hank's face. "I don't understand," Hank said, sobbing. "How can this be happening? Why would someone shoot her!"

Daniel held his dad's hand. "Mom is tough, she'll pull through!"

****

A few hours later, the doctor walked into Hank's room. They prepared themselves for the worst.

"Mr. Welch, your wife survived the surgery and we were able to stop the bleeding. She was very lucky. The bullet that entered her chest barely missed her heart. However, I need to warn you that she's not out of the woods yet. She's in grave condition and the next twenty-four hours are critical. We're transferring her to the ICU."

"Can I see her?" asked Hank.

"As soon as we have her settled, you can see her for a short time."

"I'll be right back," said James. He returned in a few minutes and let Hank know that an orderly would be taking him to see Tina once she was settled in the ICU.

"Mr. Riley, can I go with my dad?" asked Daniel.

"Of course you can."

Just then, Richards walked into the room.

"Hank and Daniel are waiting to see Tina," said James. "I really need to get home and check on the family. I think Daniel should stay at our house, but right now he needs to be here with his parents. Would it be possible for you to drop him off at our house when they are done?"

"No problem," said Richards. "Glad to help you out."

****

It was getting dark when James pulled into the driveway. He was relieved to see the patrol car still parked outside of his house.

It had been a long, disturbing day and all he wanted was a tall bourbon and water. As he walked toward the front porch Meg rushed out of the front door and wrapped her arms around James.

"I'm so glad you're home," she said. "Bob told us what happened at Hank's house. How awful."

"I hope you don't mind, but Daniel is going to stay with us. Richards is going to drop him off later this evening."

"Of course, I don't mind."

James kissed her. "Now I know why I married you."

When Ginger saw James, she ran around in circles, obviously excited to have him home.

"Wow," said Anna. "I bet you've never had so many houseguests."

"I don't mind as long as it's people that I care about," said Meg.

Clair walked over and handed her dad a bourbon and water.

"That's my girl!"

"Hey, Tom, let's go make some food," said Clair.

"I'll help," said Anna.

Sensing that Meg and James needed some alone time, Bob scooped up Ginger and joined the group in the kitchen.

Meg and James sat on the couch and held each other, savoring a few moments of quiet.

Chapter 45

Tuesday, October 3

James looked out the window when Ginger started barking. Richards and Daniel were walking up the driveway.

"Meg, Richards and Daniel are here."

Everyone came into the living room to greet them.

Richards leaned down to pet Ginger. Ginger growled and snapped at him.

"Ginger, no!" yelled James.

"That's weird," said Meg. "She's never snapped at anyone."

Meg introduced everyone. She noticed that Richards couldn't keep his eyes off of Anna. She couldn't blame Richards, he was single and Anna was stunning.

"Have a seat," said Meg. "Would you like something to drink or eat?"

"I could use a good cup of coffee," said Richards. "The coffee at the hospital is awful."

"Daniel, would you like something?" asked Meg. "How about a sandwich?"

"That sounds great, Mrs. Riley."

Daniel sat on the couch. Ginger jumped up on the couch and snuggled next to him. Daniel smiled and scratched her head.

"She sure likes you," said James.

It was at that moment that James saw the resemblance.

"I'll be right back," said Meg.

Clair and Anna followed Meg to the kitchen. When they got to the kitchen, Anna put on a pot of coffee and Clair and Meg filled a platter with sandwiches.

Tom and James brought in some kitchen chairs.

When they returned to the living room, Anna sat on the couch sandwiched between Richards and Daniel. Anna didn't seem to mind.

"Daniel, I know that your mom's parents were killed in a car accident and that she was an only child. Do you know if she had any other extended family?" asked James.

"No," said Daniel.

"Did your mom ever mention a woman named May or a man named Sven?"

"No," said Daniel. "Mr. Riley, I've taken a leave from school. I need to be here for my parents."

"I don't blame you," said James. "I don't think it's safe for you to be at school or at your house. You can stay with us for as long as you need to."

"I need to get going," said Richards. "I'll give you a call if I get any new information."

James followed Richards to his car. "When I saw Hank this morning, he mentioned that he had his gun on him the day he was attacked. Did they find it when they were clearing the crime scene?"

"I don't remember seeing it on the list. I'll check and get back to you."

Chapter 46

Wednesday, October 4

It was three in the morning and James sat in his study holding the photo of Sven. He was startled when Bob walked into the room.

"We have to stop meeting like this," said James. "Come in and close the door. I want to show you something."

He handed the photo of Sven to Bob. The family resemblance was stunning.

"Damn, this could be a picture of Daniel."

"I just realized something. Swede had piercing blue eyes. It must have been a strong gene. His children and grandson have the same eyes."

"That would go with our theory that Tina is really Kristina and Sven is Daniel's uncle," said Bob.

"I'm convinced that Sven is the one who attacked Hank and shot Tina. Until we find him, my family and friends are still in danger. We need to make sure we're the first ones to talk to Tina when she wakes up."

****

The next morning James called Richards and shared his concerns about Sven. He was relieved when Richards told him he had the same concerns and had already added additional security for Hank and Tina.

When James and Bob arrived at the hospital they decided to stop by the ICU before going to Hank's room.

Tina was still in grave condition and hadn't regained consciousness. The officer stationed outside of the ICU told them everything was quiet and that they were screening all staff and visitors going into the ICU.

When they walked into Hank's room, he was sitting up in a wheelchair.

"Looking good, my friend," said James.

"Almost feel normal," said Hank. "I sure want to get out of this place."

James grabbed a chair and sat down next to Hank. "Believe me, Hank, this is the safest place for you and Tina."

Hank held his head in his hands. "I don't understand why someone tried to kill my wife. I never discussed any details of your case with her. She doesn't know anything. What if they come after Daniel?"

"Daniel will stay with us where he will be safe."

"Thank you, James."

"Hank, I wanted to wait until you were stronger, but you

need to know what we know."

James told Hank about their trips to Seattle and San Francisco and what they had found so far. Except for one thing.

"At least we know the connection between Sven, Arturo, and Anna," said Hank.

"Hank, I haven't told you everything."

"I don't like the sound of that."

"We found Alice dead in your basement. She had suffered blunt force trauma to the back of her head."

"What the hell was she doing in my basement?"

"We believe that Alice is Tina's mother and that Sven is Tina's brother."

"That's not possible. Tina was an only child and her parents are dead."

"Hank, just listen. Tina is a nickname for Kristina. They have the same birthdate and were accountants in San Francisco during the same time period. We know that Alice was a woman consumed by hate and anger toward me and my family. She's left a trail of dead bodies. She needed money for her plan, so she killed her own sister and assumed her identity. She even used her children to help carry out her plan. I think that Tina was terrified of her mother.

"You said that you were surprised when Tina went out with you. I think that when she met you, she knew you were a good man and could keep her safe. She needed to get as far away as possible. That's why she pushed for you to transfer to the LA office.

"Another thing, we found a picture of Sven when he was Daniel's age. Daniel looks just like him."

"Then who killed Alice and tried to kill Tina?" asked Hank.

"I don't know," said James. "All I do know is that Tina knew too much and they needed to keep her from talking."

"I can't believe that my wife has been deceiving me all these years."

The nurse interrupted them. "Mr. Welch, your wife is awake. She's asking for you."

****

It was two in the afternoon and James and Bob were still at the hospital. Tom, Clair, and Daniel were in the living room watching TV. Anna wasn't feeling well and decided to take a nap. Meg decided to take advantage of a few minutes to herself and give her mother a call to make sure they were okay. She went to use the phone in their bedroom, where it was quiet.

When she picked up the receiver, someone was on the phone. It was Anna and she was talking to a man. Meg had come in on the middle of their conversation and didn't want to interrupt them, so she hung up.

As Meg came out of the bedroom, Anna was coming down the hallway.

"Anna, how are you feeling?"

"Much better."

"How about a cup of tea?"

"That would be nice."

"I hope I didn't interrupt your phone conversation. I didn't realize that you were on the phone."

"Not at all," said Anna. "I was feeling better and decided to check in with Sue to make sure everything was okay at the boutique. Sue's boyfriend, Sam, is helping her until I get back."

Meg noticed she seemed fidgety and wasn't making eye contact.

Chapter 47

Wednesday, October 4

James moved Hank's wheelchair next to Tina's bed. Hank reached over and took her hand.

Tina opened her eyes and smiled at Hank.

"I've been so worried about you. I love you and nothing will change that, but I need to ask you some questions. All you have to do is nod yes or no."

"Are you Kristina Erickson?"

Tina nodded yes.

"Did you kill your mother, Alice Erickson?"

Tears ran down her cheek. She nodded yes.

"Did she threaten you?"

She nodded yes.

"Is Sven involved in this mess?"

She nodded yes.

"Is Sven alive?"

She nodded yes.

"Who shot you?"

Before she could answer she slipped back into a deep sleep.

The nurse checked her vitals and assured Hank that Tina was okay. She was still weak and had fallen into a deep sleep, but she was stable.

"Mr. Welch, your wife needs her rest and so do you. You need to go back to your room. You can come back in a couple of hours."

"Hank, let's get you back to your room. You know that no one is going to get past the officers stationed outside of her room."

"James, I can't believe that Tina was part of this plan to destroy your family. My job is to get the criminals. Hell, I was living with one!"

"Hank, it's not your fault. I don't blame Tina, she was brainwashed by her mother. To her credit, she must have wanted out. In spite of her mother, she found love and security with you and Daniel. If she did kill Alice, I am convinced that it was self-defense."

"I guess you're right."

"We need to find Sven," said Hank. "There still could be other players."

"It's possible," said James. "Someone still wants to hurt my family. Most of the suspects are dead and we can rule out Tina and Alice."

James looked at his watch, it was almost six. "Bob and I are going to go back to my house and let you get some rest. Don't worry, Hank, we'll figure this out."

"I know you will. When Tina wakes up, I'll try to get more information on Sven."

Chapter 48

Wednesday, October 4

James sped down the freeway, anxious to get home. Fortunately, they had missed the rush-hour traffic.

"Bob, remember when I suspected that the prowler I chased from my house and the guy who I chased out of the FBI garage could be the same guy? What if it was a woman?"

"What makes you think that?"

"Just a gut feeling. I need to find a pay phone."

James pulled off the freeway and found a pay phone at a gas station.

He needed to know if Anna or Arturo had participated in track and field events in high school. He also wanted to know if she owned a gun. He called Richards' office, but he wasn't there. James was put through to Agent Cooper, who had recovered from the head injury he suffered the night that Arturo broke into James' house.

James relayed his message to Cooper, who assured him he would forward the message to Richards.

James returned to the car. "Hey, Bob, ready for a nice strong highball and some food?"

"Sounds good to me."

Chapter 49

Wednesday, October 4

It was finally beginning to feel like autumn. The Santa Ana winds had stopped. The days were in the mid-seventies and the nights were in the high fifties. People from the East Coast claimed that California didn't have seasons. They were wrong. California just had all the seasons throughout the year.

James and Bob could smell Meg's chili as soon as they got out of the car.

Meg met them at the door, a highball in each hand.

"You're one lucky man," said Bob.

When they finished dinner, Meg asked James to help her clean the kitchen. She said that it was to give Clair a break, but he knew her too well. She only let him work in her kitchen when she needed to talk to him privately.

"Okay, Meg, what's on your mind?"

She gave him a kiss. "I need to tell you something. I overheard Anna on the phone with a man. His voice sounded familiar."

Meg repeated Anna's explanation. "I don't believe her," she added.

James knew Meg was an excellent judge of character and that she could smell a lie a mile away.

Chapter 50

Friday, October 6

It was three in the morning and James was still awake. So far, the investigation had left them with more questions than answers. He needed to take another look at all the evidence and people involved in the investigation. He slowly rolled out of bed, trying not to disturb Meg.

Meg sat up. "Are you okay?"

"I'm fine, just can't sleep. I'm going to work in my study."

"You mean to work on the investigation."

"I just need to put everything in perspective. Maybe it will help our suspect list."

"Do you need my help?"

"Not right now. You go back to sleep."

****

Bob walked into his office. "I got up to use the bathroom and saw the light under the door. You okay?"

"Just taking another look at the details of the case. Want to join me?"

"You bet."

As they went through the evidence, they noted all the key people involved in the investigation.

"We know that Alice started her plan when Swede was killed in 1940," James said. "She filled her children with her hate and a thirst for revenge. She killed her only sister so she could steal her money and identity.

"Sven would have been easier for Alice to manipulate. He loved his father and would have easily bought into Alice's plan for revenge.

"Tina's been victimized by her mother from the day she was born. She never knew her father. Without an emotional attachment to Swede, she didn't have the thirst for revenge. She'd lived with an awful secret her whole life. When she tried to start a new life and distance herself from Sven and Alice, they threatened her family.

"I'm almost sure that Alice attacked Hank. I'm guessing, when Tina found out, she confronted her. They argued and all the rage she had bottled up over the years finally boiled over. Tina picked up the first thing she found and hit her. Probably a crowbar or pipe. Realizing that her fingerprints were on the weapon, she got rid of it."

"What happened to Tina at the hospital?" asked Bob.

"I think Tina left on her own to confront Alice about Hank and left the syringe to make us think that she had been abducted.

Maybe it was a clue for us to go to the house so we could catch Alice and free her from this mess. Unfortunately, we got there too late."

"I'm really convinced that Anna is our missing link. Anna and Arturo are linked to Alice and Sven. I don't think it was a coincidence that Anna just happened to stop at the house in San Francisco the day we showed up. I think she was living there with Sven and Alice and she knew the whole sordid story. I'm sure she was looking for something specific in that basement. She seemed surprised when she found out that May was actually Alice, but I'm sure it was an act. I wonder how much money they offered her to work with them?"

Bob spoke up. "What about Daniel?"

"I'm not sure. I hope that Daniel isn't involved. I just can't get past the fact that he arrived at the house right after his mother was shot."

"He's been to see his parents," said Bob.

"That could be a way to throw us off the track. It's a wait and see on Daniel."

They stopped talking when they heard the hardwood floor creak outside of the study door.

James walked over and opened the door.

Whoever it was, he or she was gone.

Chapter 51

Friday, October 6

Later that morning, James received a call from Richards.

"Sorry I missed your call. Had to take care of some personal business."

He told Richards about Meg overhearing Anna on the phone with a man.

"I got the information on Anna. I checked with the high school in New York. She and Arturo both participated in track and field. Anna was actually better than her brother. I couldn't find a gun registered to Anna or Arturo. Of course, we both know they could have gotten a gun illegally."

"What about Sam and Sue?"

"I'm still waiting."

James went over the list of suspects. He told him they were sure that someone had been listening at the study door.

"I think it's time to get everyone together. How about tonight?"

"Why don't you come over for dinner around six?"

****

When Richards arrived, he pulled James to the side. "My guys in San Francisco just got back to me. They went to the boutique about an hour ago and found Sue's body; she'd been strangled. It didn't appear to be a robbery. There was still money in the cash register and nothing was out of place.

"The coroner estimated she had been dead for at least twenty-four hours. They checked with some of the neighboring business owners. No one remembered Sue having a boyfriend or seeing a man working at the boutique.

"However, the owner of the café next door said he had gone into the boutique around five to see if Sue wanted to order some dinner. He said a man was in the boutique with Sue and he assumed that the man was a customer. Sue told him she would be closing soon and would stop by to order some food. He said he got the feeling she wanted him to leave. He said the man appeared to be in his thirties and that he had cold, piercing blue eyes. Gave him the creeps.

"When Sue didn't show at the restaurant by six, he went to check on her. He said the boutique was locked up and the closed sign was in the window. He was devastated when he found out she had been murdered. He said she was a real nice girl, not snooty like the other owner, Anna."

"The guy in the boutique had to be Sven," said James.

Richards agreed. "James, if he caught a flight out of San

Francisco, he's here and waiting for his chance to get to you."

"We need to put some pressure on Anna and Daniel."

****

James, Richards, and Bob agreed on seating arrangements at the dinner table.

"We need to make sure that Anna and Daniel are covered," said Richards. "We can put them on the left side of the table that backs up to the wall. I'll sit between them."

"I'll sit at the head of the table, so Anna and Daniel will be to my left," said James. "Bob, you'll sit at the other end of the table. Meg, Clair, and Tom on the right side of the table."

When they entered the dining room, Meg had placed name cards on the table. "Everyone has been so stressed, I thought it would be nice to have dinner in the dining room," she said.

Daniel ignored the name cards and went for the chair next to Anna.

Richards cut him off. "Sorry, buddy, this is my seat."

Daniel pulled his chair out so hard that it hit the wall. He slumped down in the chair and crossed his arms.

Anna and Daniel picked at their food.

When they finished dinner, Anna started to get up from the table.

"Anna, sit down," said James.

"I don't feel well," she said.

"I apologize, but I need everyone to stay where they are. Anna, I have some questions for you."

"You told us that the people on the phone, on Wednesday, were Sue and her boyfriend, Sam."

"That's right. I had to check on the boutique!"

"I'm sorry to tell you they found Sue's body at the boutique today; she was murdered."

James wasn't surprised when Anna didn't act upset and didn't ask how she died.

"What's really strange, none of the business owners remember ever seeing a man working with Sue at the boutique. However, the café owner next door to the boutique saw a man in the boutique shortly before Sue was murdered. A man with piercing blue eyes."

Anna just sat there, glaring at James.

"I'm guessing that you don't have to ask how she was murdered because you already know."

"Sue started putting the pieces together," Anna confessed. "I was impressed, since she never displayed much intelligence, but she had to go."

Daniel started to jump up from his chair. He was no match for Bob, who shoved him back in his chair. Richards pulled out two sets of handcuffs. Tom helped Richards shackle Daniel's hands and ankles.

"Daniel, did you shoot your mother?" James asked.

"Daniel, shut your mouth!" Anna yelled.

Suddenly, Daniel looked very young. Tears welled up in his eyes. "They told me that my mom was a traitor to the family and that she killed my grandmother."

"Daniel, where is Sven?"

"I swear, I don't know!"

"When was the last time you saw him?"

"The day I shot my mom."

Anna started to stand up. James pushed her back into the chair.

"You idiot!" yelled Anna. "You're weak, just like your mother."

Richards grabbed Anna by the shoulders. "One more outburst from you and I'll tape your mouth shut!"

They used James' belt to restrain Anna.

"Daniel, right now you're looking at being charged with attempted murder. You're seventeen and the DA could agree to have you tried as a juvenile. However, if your mother dies, you will be charged with first-degree murder. I'm pretty sure the DA will charge you as an adult and, if convicted, you could be facing the death penalty.

"If you cooperate with us, we might be able to convince the DA there were special circumstances that led to your actions, such as your age and the fact that you would have never tried to murder your mother, had it not been for Alice and Sven. They took advantage of a young boy who was easy to manipulate. What's your answer?"

"I'll tell you what I know."

"Where is Sven?"

Anna interrupted. "You're never going to find him. When Sven was discharged from the military, he moved to San Francisco and became involved in a community theater group. He became a master of disguise. Wigs, makeup, and contact lenses. Actors have been using them for years to change their eye color or make someone appear to be blind. Blue eyes can be changed to brown eyes in an instant."

"Since you're being so chatty, can you tell me what you were really looking for in Alice's basement?"

"Sorry, I'm done talking."

****

They watched as they put Daniel and Anna in the squad car. They would be held at the holding cell at the Monrovia PD, until they could be transferred to a LA County facility.

Richards walked over to James and Bob. "I'm going to follow them to the police station; I want to make sure they get there. I'll be back in a couple of hours. Agent Cooper and Agent Stevens will be covering the alley behind your house."

James shook Cooper's hand. "Good to see you, Agent Cooper."

"This is Agent Stevens," said Cooper. "He just transferred to our office."

"Glad to have you on board," said James. "You guys be careful out there tonight."

****

Although they had additional agents watching the house and Anna and Daniel were safely incarcerated, James knew they couldn't let their guard down. As long as Sven was out there, they were in danger. That night they all stayed in the living room. Unfortunately, there was only one extra gun and that went to Bob. The only weapon they were able to find for Tom was a baseball bat. Since Tom hadn't had much experience with firearms, it worked for him.

Meg and Clair were on the couch. Meg had a flashlight. She put a leash on Ginger just in case they had to make a quick exit. Tom sat in a chair next to the couch. James covered the front door and Bob covered the back door.

Tom stood up. "I'll be right back."

****

Richards stayed with Daniel and Anna until they were put in the holding cells.

He started to leave when an officer stopped him. "Agent Richards, you have an urgent call from your office."

Chapter 52

They were startled when the phone rang. Before James could answer, Bob and Agent Stevens walked into the living room.

"Don't answer the phone!" yelled Stevens. "I have a gun pointed at your friend and I won't hesitate to use it."

"Sorry, James," said Bob. "I really screwed up."

"James, I need you to put your gun on the floor."

What Stevens didn't know was that Tom was behind them and he had the baseball bat.

James needed to keep Stevens focused on his gun.

"Now, kick the gun over to me."

As James moved toward the gun, he nodded to Tom.

Tom swung the bat, hitting Stevens in the arm and knocking the gun out of his hand. Then he hit him in the back of the legs. Stevens screamed in agony and fell to the floor. Tom's next target was his head, but James stopped him.

"It's okay, Tom. We need him alive."

"Meg, get my handcuffs."

Tom leaned over to Stevens.

"Don't you ever try to hurt my family!"

Clair ran over to Tom. "You saved us."

"Tom, where did you come from?" asked Bob.

"I was coming down the hallway from the bathroom. When I got to the doorway to the kitchen, I saw you and Stevens walking through the kitchen. The look on your face told me something was wrong and I moved back so you couldn't see me. When you passed by me, I saw that Stevens had his gun pressed against your back. I couldn't get to the living room to warn the others. Fortunately, I had the baseball bat."

"I owe you, my friend," said Bob.

As James walked over to Stevens, he noticed that Stevens had one brown eye and one blue eye.

"Well, Sven, we finally meet. I think you lost one of your contact lenses."

****

Richards told James he had gotten a call alerting him they had found the real Agent Stevens in his apartment, bound and gagged.

"I knew it had to be Sven. Stevens had just transferred to our office and this would have been his first assignment. Sven only needed to impersonate Stevens for one night."

"When I tried to call and you didn't answer, I knew you were in trouble. I couldn't radio the agents watching your house without alerting Sven. I didn't know what I would find when I got here."

"Tom was our hero," said James. "He took Sven down with a baseball bat."

"Is Cooper okay?" asked James.

"He's fine," said Richards. "Sven must have put something in his coffee that knocked him out. He's still a little groggy."

"I'm so thankful that my family is safe," said James.

Chapter 53

James and Meg had been on a roller coaster of emotions so long they had almost forgotten how to relax. They sat by the pool enjoying a cocktail, thankful their nightmare was finally over.

Clair and Tom had returned to Ohio to sell their house and prepare for their move to California. It wasn't a surprise they decided against the old Victorian house. They did find another house in the neighborhood. It needed some work, but nothing that James and Tom couldn't handle.

Bob wanted to start writing true crime novels and had decided to relocate to LA. James and Meg were looking forward to having him back in their lives.

Hank's family had a lot of healing ahead of them. Hank had been released from the hospital and James and Meg had insisted he stay with them until he was stronger.

Tina was making progress. She had been moved to a skilled nursing facility, where she could receive intensive physical therapy. Hank hoped that by the time she was ready to come home, he would be able to take care of her.

Tina wasn't charged with Alice's death. The coroner was able to confirm that Alice didn't die from the first blow to the head. In fact, all she had was a bump on the back of her head. Sven confessed that Alice was still alive when he returned to Hank's house. They argued, he picked up a steel pipe, and beat her in the head until she died.

The DA had gone with Richards' recommendation to charge Daniel as a juvenile. The judge ruled that Daniel suffered from serious emotional issues that required intensive therapy and he was placed in a mental facility. Hank and Tina hoped that someday Daniel would recover and be able to live a normal life.

Anna made a deal to testify against Sven and was sentenced to twenty years to life as an accessory to murder.

Sven was convicted of the murders of his mother, Alice, Red McCoy, Virgil Potter, and Sue Ross. He was sentenced to the death penalty.

Acknowledgements

Thank you to my husband and children for their continued love and support.

Thank you to former FBI agents, Thomas Jourdan, PHD and Neal Hunt, for taking time out of your busy schedules to answer my questions.

Thank you to my beta readers, Jan Woolford, Sandy Burnett and Betty Tabor.